Emily Sarah Holt

John de Wycliffe

The First of the Reformers and What he Did for England

Emily Sarah Holt

John de Wycliffe
The First of the Reformers and What he Did for England

ISBN/EAN: 9783337296803

Printed in Europe, USA, Canada, Australia, Japan

Cover: Foto ©Raphael Reischuk / pixelio.de

More available books at **www.hansebooks.com**

JOHN DE WYCLIFFE

Ꭲꜧe First of the Reformers,

AND

WHAT HE DID FOR ENGLAND.

BY

EMILY S. HOLT,

AUTHOR OF "MISTRESS MARGERY," "SISTER ROSE,"
"IMOGEN," ETC.

LONDON:

JOHN F. SHAW AND Co.,

48, PATERNOSTER ROW, E.C.

CONTENTS.

JOHN DE WYCLIFFE.

CHAPTER I.

N the moral world, no less than the physical, there is a succession of ages. The Golden Age comes first, when the heroes are the builders, inventors, and artificers, the Nimrods, the Jubals, and the Tubal-cains. Then follows the Stone Age, when the men most admired are kings and warriors ; and this commonly lasts long. After it is the Iron Age, when the thinkers come into prominence—the philosophers, the reformers, and the martyrs. And last of all comes a fourth age, which has received no name—shall we call it the Porcelain Age ? seeing that its products are mostly of a fragile yet elaborate character, and its heroes are the men who amuse the languid world—artists, musicians, actors, and dancers. And when this last age has fairly set in—not as an occasional episode to the others, but as a moral tone pervading

the whole of society—the ruin of that country which it has infected cannot be far off.

Some men are famous only while they live, and are scarcely heard of afterwards. Some, who were hardly known while they lived, become very famous afterwards. And for some of this latter class, the afterwards is long in coming; centuries may go by, and the world seems to have forgotten them. But at last some discovery bursts upon a following age, and it awakes to find out that such a man was a hero, though he might be no prophet in his own country or century, and the green moss of many a year may have obliterated his epitaph. Not seldom are such men regarded as the reverse of heroes while they are alive. Their own world at least disdains, if it do not revile and persecute them. There have not been many in the ranks of those of whom the world was not worthy, whom the world as they were passing through thought at all worthy of it.

John Wycliffe was one of those men whose fame has tarried behind them, and whose good deeds have followed them long afterwards. He was not without fame in his own day, but the distinction which he enjoyed was chiefly that of being scorned and hated. So long as he was only known as a scholar, the world respected him; when at a later period he came forth as a statesman, the world honoured him; but when he took up a third character, and began to try to make the world a little better than he had found it, then the world could not forgive him. It rarely does pardon that capital offence. If it can find a fault in such persons, trust the world to do it ; and if their walk through God's grace be so far blameless that it can find no occasion against them, except it find it concerning the law of their God, then it hates them without a cause, and dubs them saints, enthusi-asts, Methodists, or whatever other opprobrious term may happen to be in its favour at the time.

The chief reason why the fame of Wycliffe has been eclipsed by that of Luther is that the one succeeded in achieving the aim of his life far more rapidly and openly than the other. Something may be due to the fact that Luther was the more single-eyed of the two, and also the more energetic and determined. To use a hackneyed simile, he had " fewer irons in the fire." His way was not encum-bered by much of the intellectual machinery which stood in that of Wycliffe, nor by any of those traditions of position and conventionality which, like the relics of broken fetters, clung to and weakened the hands of the earlier Reformer. Luther set before him one grand aim, and shot away persistently until he hit it. He saw that the stream was turbid, and he went and cleaned out the fountain. Wycliffe's strength was somewhat distracted by having a greater number of aims, and by trying to purify the stream, if possible, without meddling quite so much with the fountain. It was not possible, and both of them found it out; but had Wycliffe made the discovery as early in his career as Luther, it is probable—looking to second causes—that the Reformation would have come two

B 2

hundred and fifty years sooner than it did. And yet, though Luther has achieved the higher fame, there is a sense in which Wycliffe was the greater reformer of the two. His work was of a more difficult character, and he made fewer blunders in the doing of it. He did not give hasty slashes to Gordian knots, and then find that he had made a mistake and had to tie them up again, or, worse still, that the mistake had been made, and the knot could not be tied again. He walked more slowly and carefully along the dangerous road ; but the impulsive, determined runner won the race, and the graver and more cautious pilgrim did not live to reach the goal. The goal was reached at last, but it was not by him, nor for many a year after his ashes had been scattered upon the waters of the Avon. But the pioneers of the forest clearing are the men without whom the city in its strength and grandeur would never be able to arise. The architect and the mason may see the city in its glory, but the woodman who cuts away the brushwood and hews down the trees rarely survives long enough to do so. Yet, as a German philosopher has remarked, "it very often happens that efforts which seem to have perished with those who made them, exercise a more enduring influence upon subsequent events than the conqueror who prematurely triumphs."

Both English and German Reformer came of Teutonic blood. In the case of Wycliffe, there was not improbably a little Scandinavian admixture. There are two places in England known by his name, but the northern one in Yorkshire is Wycliffe, and the more southern, in Northamptonshire, is Wyclive. John Wycliffe the Reformer was one of those sturdy Yorkshiremen, slow, shrewd, and sure, whose character forms the moral backbone of England as their border-land does the physical one.

On the southern bank of the Tees, and at the very edge of the North Riding, where the county of York joins that of Durham, in a fair and fertile valley of remarkable loveliness, with grand rugged hills on every side, lies the little village of Wycliffe, so small that it has no place in the Postal Guide; and its population in 1853 was less than two hundred souls. The church is towerless, and partially covered with ivy; and on a high bank near it stands the old manor-house, the family seat of the ancient lords of Wycliffe. Except in the female line, the family has died out. The last male of the old house died about the beginning of the seventeenth century, and, strange to say, down to the last, the lords of Wycliffe Manor remained Romanists. The little Romish chapel, which on Sundays holds about half the inhabitants of the little village, stands on the high bank by the side of the manor-house. The prophet was least of all accepted in his own country. But the family has not perished without leaving its mark on history, for its one son who rose to eminence became famous in many lands and for all time.

While etymology long ago settled the spelling of Luther's name—a very uncertain matter in his own day—the name of the English Reformer continues to be spelt according to the pleasure of the writer. With

Professor Lechler he is Wiclif; with Mr. Arnold, the editor of his English works, Wyclif, which latter spelling has also been adopted by the society which bears his name. The contemporary Bohemian transcribers of his works are sorely puzzled to spell it; they give us Wygleph, Vikleph, and even Wyclifficek. In the State Papers of his own day, we find him thrice as Wyclif, twice as Wyclyf, and once as Wiclyf. The name of the village whence that of the man is derived has settled down into Wycliffe, and it seems to me that the name of the Reformer should follow the same rule.

Beyond the fact that he rose from the ranks of the landed gentry, nothing is known with certainty of the relatives of John Wycliffe. There is, however, one further probability—that he was the son of a younger son, and as such had to be the architect of his own fortunes. It is probable that his father was not lord of the manor, because he was not born in the manorhouse, but in the adjoining village of Spresswell, about half a mile distant, and now no longer in existence. The year of his birth is nowhere on record. The one usually assigned to it is 1324, which was fixed upon by one of his earliest biographers, as it appears for no special reason beyond a vague impression that the Reformer was about sixty at the time of his death. It is, however, likely that this is about the true date. Circumstances seem to show that Wycliffe could not well be much younger than this; and at a time when fifty was the average duration of human life, and a man who passed sixty was regarded as far advanced in age, it is improbable that he was much, if any older.

That any man can be the architect of his own fortunes is of course true only in a secondary sense. Of every man's career in this world God is the chief architect, and the man is only a day-labourer under Him. But there are some careers in which this fact is permitted to appear more patently than in others. In some cases we see only the day-labourer, patiently working away, stroke after stroke, and the plan of the great Architect is hidden from us. In others there are, as it were, stopping-places, where the tools are taken out of the labourer's hand, and the Architect permits Himself to be seen as He directs the work. One of these latter instances was the life of John Wycliffe.

According to the usual custom of his day, the boy would receive his first education, after leaving his mother's side, at the hands of the parish priest. Who this was cannot be stated. About forty years later, we find that two priests of this parish were themselves Wycliffes ; and it is extremely probable that one son of the family was usually brought up for the priest-hood, and occupied the village benefice. It is not unlikely, therefore, that young John's tutor was a relative of his own, and the idea of his family in sending him to the university and training him for the priesthood, may have been that he should succeed to the family living in due time. But God destined John Wycliffe for very different work.

It would have been interesting if we could have

known more of Wycliffe's parents. Had he a self-
sacrificing father, who allowed himself few of the
luxuries of his day, while he scraped together the
money necessary to send his studious boy to Oxford ?
—or an anxious, praying mother, who gave many a
sigh and hope to her clever Jack, wondering if he
would be a credit to her when he had passed out of
her sight ? Or was he early left an orphan, thrown
on the care of an uncle or cousin at Wycliffe Manor,
who thought he had done his duty by sending the lad
off to college, and that no more could be expected of
him ? All that we know is, that till he was about
fifteen, the future Reformer dwelt among the grand,
rugged hills of Richmondshire, and in the fair and
fertile vale of the silver Tees—and that (with one
possibly exceptional instance to which allusion will
presently be made in its due chronological place)
when once he turned away from his native mountains,
he seems to have turned back no more.

It was probably about 1338, or 1340, that the boy
was sent up to Oxford. The universities at that date
more nearly resembled foreign universities than they
now do, combining the true college with the public
school. Boys were sent to Oxford or Cambridge
even so early as the age of ten. The probable age
of Cardinal Beaufort when sent to college was nine
years ; twelve is the utmost he can possibly have
been. If the tradition be true—it is not likely—which
states that Wycliffe was first entered at Queen's, he
cannot have gone up before 1340, since that was the
year when the college came into existence.

Three colleges contend for the honour of his education, Queen's, Merton, and Balliol. Of these there
can be little doubt that Balliol has the best claim,
and that his connection with both the others (the
latter being somewhat uncertain) belongs to a later
period of his life. Balliol was the college to which a
youth coming from Richmondshire would naturally
be sent, for it was founded by Dervorgoil de Baliol,
Lady of Barnard's Castle, the stately towers of which
rose on the opposite bank of the Tees, only five or six
miles from Wycliffe.

At that time a custom prevailed in the University
of Oxford, and indeed in most others, by which the
students were divided into "nations" according to
their birth-places. Four was the usual number, but
at Oxford there were only two, *Boreales* and *Australes*,
or Northerners and Southerners. Wycliffe, as might
be guessed, was a Northerner.

The course of study then pursued in the universities
was of a wider character than now with respect to
science, and of a narrower with regard to languages.
Latin was then, as now, the tongue of the learned ;
but Greek was all but unknown, and for a man to
express a wish for the study of Hebrew would have
been thought little short of insanity. The modern
languages were not taught at all ; but it must not
be forgotten that every person who had any claim
to gentle blood had spoken French from his in-
fancy as a matter of course. The point of doubt
as between the two languages, would be whether
he knew English. It was only about 1370—some

thirty years later—that educated Englishmen began
to use their own language as a means of common
intercourse.

The grand curriculum of education at that time was
known by the name of the Seven Sciences. Three of
these—grammar, logic, and rhetoric—constituted the
Trivium, roughly known as "logic" in conventional
speech; the less learned portion of the students did
not pass beyond these. The remaining sciences—arith-
metic, geometry, astronomy, and music, were termed
the *Quadrivium*, and more generally "physics." The
one of these various sciences held in the greatest
esteem was logic, and in this department of learning
Wycliffe became an adept; but his personal taste
appears to have led him rather to natural philosophy
in all its branches. Optics and acoustics, chemistry
and mathematics, were his favourite pursuits; and
from them he draws his illustrations freely, not only
in Latin discourses addressed to the learned, but in
his English sermons intended for the simple. Yet
beyond all these, in the eyes of the public, and
doubtless in those of Wycliffe, rose another science, at
that time regarded as the queen of the sciences, and
certain to form the surest stepping-stone to fame and
honour which it was possible to attain. This was
theology. It is not known whether Wycliffe's friends
from the first intended him for the priesthood, or
whether his own choice led him in that direction;
but it seems probable, in the latter case, that his
motive was rather an intellectual one, than either of
an ambitious or a religious character. His thirst

for knowledge of all kinds appears to have been intense.

The usual course of study allotted two years to the *Trivium*, two to the *Quadrivium*, and seven to theology. But theology, as then understood, was not the same study as now. Lectures on the Bible itself were entrusted to the lowest class of tutors,. and were regarded as a mere preparation for the more important subjects which were to follow. Any knowledge, not merely of the original tongues, Hebrew and Greek, but of the antiquities, the manners and customs, and the natural history, of Bible lands was totally out of the question. The Vulgate or Latin translation of the Bible was the only form of Scripture within reach ; and the doctors of the University regarded it as completely beneath their dignity to occupy themselves with what they considered such mere elementary work. The inter-pretation of the Bible, too, was confined within certain hard and fast rules, absurdly termed "the consent of the Fathers,"[1] and no explanation of

---

[1] It may be as well to give one or two instances of this style of Scriptural comment, since few Protestants understand what it really is. The Church of Rome to this day holds, as a consequence of the rule referred to, that because Christ said to Peter only, " Launch out into the deep," and merely commanded the other apostles to leave their nets, therefore the Pope alone, as Peter's successor, is qualified to decide questions of faith and practice ; and because He said to John, " Behold thy mother," therefore every Christian is to look on the Virgin Mary in the light of his own mother ! These are facts, however like insanities they may look to plain Protestant eyes.

the simplest point was admitted which did not
agree with these. No man might think for himself
in the fourteenth century as to religious matters.
He must either think with the Church, or must
prepare to be ostracized from society and severely
punished for heresy. And it was the boast of
England, though not quite a true one, that her stream
of " Catholic doctrine " had been kept pure and
undefiled from any of those sewers of heresy which
had polluted the theological rivers of the continent.
When a man had passed through this primary
course at the hands of the *biblici*, or lower rank of
theological tutors who lectured on Scripture, he was
transferred to the classes of the *sententiarii*, or higher
rank of the lecturers on scholastic theology. He
now studied the writings of the Fathers, the canon law
of the Church, and more especially the "sentences"
of Peter Lombard, who was considered the supreme
authority in this science. The minor works chiefly
in favour at this time were, the *Summa* of Thomas
Aquinas, the works of Bishop Grosteste of Lincoln,
and the book of Archbishop Fitzralph of Armagh
against the errors of the Armenian Church.

Another point which is known to have engaged
Wycliffe's attention was the great quarrel then raging
between the Realists and Nominalists. All the northerners were Realists, all the southerners Nominalists.
It may be said, to give as short an explanation as
possible, that this was simply the modern question
of objective *versus* subjective, or what the Germans
term the *Ich* and the *Nicht Ich*. Does anything

exist in reality, apart from the operations of the human mind, or does nothing exist except as appre-hended by the human mind? Do the common articles in daily use—the fire, the chair, the book—really exist apart from me, the person seeing them, or have they no existence outside my imagination? Plain people are apt to think that if two or more pairs of eyes can see a thing, the thing must be there to see; but the schoolmen were not plain people at all, but people of very knotty and analy-tical minds. This, then, was the grand question, to which the Realists answered that there was such an existence, and the Nominalists contended that there was not. Balliol College was the stronghold of the Realists, who claimed their founder, John Scott, commonly called Duns Scotus, as a Balliol man. Beyond the question itself, which is still fully alive in the East, and in Europe has survived in a mild form to the present day—for Oxford under-graduates no longer fight pitched battles in Logic Lane upon the subject—a relic of this great middle-age contest remains in the word *dunce*, the oppro-brious term, taken from the name of their founder, which was fixed upon the Realists by their opponents.

From 1340 to 1361 the life of our Reformer is almost blank of any records. Only a few skeleton facts stand out, themselves the more uncertain because they seem at variance with each other, and also because there were at this time two John Wycliffes at Oxford, and it is extremely difficult to judge which of them is the one intended. Some

writers have contended that there was only one
such person, but the evidence makes this impossible.
Some have supposed that the other John Wycliffe
was a relative of the Reformer, and a Wycliffe of
Wycliffe ; but the fact that the name of the former
is generally spelt Wyclyve, Whytclyfe, or Whitcliff,
fails to confirm this supposition. Only in two contemporary instances is the name of the Reformer
spelt Wycleve (where it is certain to be his) ; and
these are in the Bishop of Lincoln's register, the
scribe of which would be almost sure to spell the
name in that form familiar to himself. In all other
instances the Reformer is Wiclef, Wiclyf, Wyclif, or
Wicliffe, spelt in the same manner as the village which
was the seat of the family. There is no necessity to
pursue the career of this other John Wyclyve further
than just sufficiently to avoid identifying him with
his greater namesake. He it is supposed to have
been, and not the Reformer, who was appointed
parish priest of Mayfield, in Sussex, by Archbishop
Islip, on the 20th of July, 1361, and was in 1380
transferred to the neighbouring parish of Horsted
Keynes ; he was made a prebendary in the cathedral
of Chichester, died in November, 1383, just one
year earlier than the Reformer, and was buried at
Maidstone.[1] It is, however, a much more doubtful
question which of them was Fellow and Seneschal
of Merton in 1356, and which was appointed by

[1] Ducarel's Registers of the Archbishops of Canterbury,
Additional MS. 6073, fol. 763. Wyclyf is the spelling in
his will.

Archbishop Islip to the wardenship of Canterbury Hall in 1365. In the account here given, the most trustworthy authorities have been followed, and by them the Wycliffe of Merton is believed to have been Wyclyve of Mayfield,[1] and the Wycliffe of Canterbury Hall to have been the Reformer.

A careful weighing of all the circumstances of the case renders it probable that Wycliffe remained entirely at Balliol until he was appointed Master of that college. The exact date of this promotion is not on record ; it was not earlier than 1357, nor later than 1360. It was for no long time that he occupied this position. On the 16th of May, 1361, his college presented him to the rectory of Filling-ham, a small parish about ten miles to the north-west of Lincoln. He was still Master of Balliol in the subsequent July, but in October, 1363, he appears to have resigned the post, as he is then found living in rooms at Queen's College.

To this portion of Wycliffe's life belongs a passing allusion to *a* John Wycliffe, which, if it refer to our Reformer—and that is doubtful—is of some interest to his biography. This is an entry on the Issue Roll for Easter, 1362, of a payment made, June 14th, to Richard de Tempest, custodian of the town of Berwick-upon-Tweed, of £125, for official purposes, " by the hands of John Wyclif." There is no proof

---

[1] Additional probability is imparted to this belief from the fact recently discovered that Oxford was at that time rent by factions, Balliol being the stronghold of one and Merton of the other. A Fellow of Merton was the last person likely to be elected Master of Balliol.

that this is our John Wycliffe, especially since he is
not described as " clerk "; and it may reasonably be
urged that the Master of Balliol and Rector of
Fillingham was not very likely to be making journeys
to Berwick. On the other hand, the entry may
indicate a solitary visit paid by the Oxford Don to
his old Richmond hills and far-off kinsfolk, combined
with a confidential journey further north, by command of King Edward III., who certainly respected
and trusted Wycliffe, perhaps not merely to deliver
a sum of money, but to carry some grave information or secret orders to the keeper of Berwick, too
important to be trusted to any meaner hand.

The fourteenth century was an age of pluralities.
The famous William de Wykeham held no less
than twelve livings, on none of which he resided,
since he was obliged to live continually at Court as
private secretary to the King. Hereafter, John
Wycliffe was to fight manfully against pluralities;
but it is unlikely that his future opinions on the
question had dawned upon his mind so early
as 1361. It may be considered very doubtful
whether he ever lived at Fillingham in term time,
though he may perhaps have spent the vacations
there. It is, in fact, a certainty that on the 13th of
April, 1368, licence for non-residence was granted to
him by the Bishop of Lincoln, for two years, in
order to devote himself more completely to his
studies at the University. But whether this licence
were exceptional, or one of a series of similar documents, I leave to the reader's judgment. The

latter solution appears the less probable when we find that in November, 1368, Wycliffe exchanged his benefice of Fillingham, for that of Ludgershall, in Buckinghamshire, the latter being much nearer Oxford than the former.

But before this last event happened, Wycliffe's academical status and abode had undergone another change. Simon de Islip, Archbishop of Canterbury, founded a new college at Oxford, to which he gave the name of Canterbury Hall. It is now merged in Christ Church, one of whose gates and quadrangles still retain the name of Canterbury. The person whom the Archbishop selected as his first warden was a monk named Woodhall, whose violent temper seems to have acted unhappily upon his scholars, and the new Hall became a perpetual scene of unedifying quarrels. Finding this, the Archbishop deposed Woodhall, and appointed, Dec. 9th, 1365, "John Wyclyve" to the mastership of his college.[1] It is still to some extent an open question whether this were the Reformer or his namesake ; and oddly enough, Wycliffe himself refers to the transaction in his treatise *De Ecclesia,* but in terms so vague that it is impossible to decide whether he speaks of himself or of another person. There is strong circumstantial evidence on both sides ; but in the present state of knowledge regarding Wycliffe's life, it appears to be

[1] Hall appears to have been at that date the ordinary term in English for a college. "Our college called Mi eluniuersitehall at Oxford," and "Our college called la Quenehalle at Oxford" occur on the Close Rolls as indicating University and Queen's Colleges.

rather stronger on the affirmative than the negative side. He must, therefore, be regarded as the Warden of Canterbury Hall, unless fresh testimony should be discovered to show that this was not the case.

In appointing his old friend to this office—for they had been fellow-students — the Archbishop specially indicates his reasons for the choice, as being the new warden's " learning and estimable life, his practical qualifications of fidelity, circumspection and diligence." For legal and technical reasons into which it is not needful to enter, it appears that this appointment was contrary to the foundation statutes, but was made by the founder himself with the assent of the Crown. But only five months later (April 26th, 1366) the good Archbishop Islip died ; and his successor, Simon Langham, who was translated from Ely, was a man cast in very different mould. His first act on his elevation was to remove Wycliffe from the wardenship. Only six days after his enthroniza-tion he appointed a new warden, and the deposition of the previous warden must of course have preceded this appointment. Three weeks later, the Archbishop deposed his new warden, and restored the original one, Henry Woodhall, whose tyrannical rule had already so perturbed the college.

It is the more necessary to state these facts in detail, since in Wycliffe's after life his enemies made considerable capital out of them. They accused him not only of insubordinate conduct under the original warden, and of plotting to remove him from his place, but they intimate not obscurely that his attacks on the friars are entirely due to spite, because the monks in the college had taken the part of Woodhall, who was one of themselves—the officials of the college consisting of a mixture of monks and secular priests ; and also that his opposition to the Papacy proceeded from his mortification at the failure of his appeal to the Pope, who in 1370 rejected Wycliffe's suit, and confirmed the restoration of Woodhall. It is only necessary in reply to remark that Wycliffe's " Four Sects," against whom his opposition was made, included canons and rich secular clergy, as well as monks and friars ; that his reformation, as has always been the case in this country, was political first, and religious afterwards ; that his opposition to the friars did not commence before 1377 at the earliest,—Professor Lechler, "the master of Wycliffe-research," considers that it was not until 1381 ; and that his war against the Papacy was a matter of slow and gradual progress—not a sudden blow struck without premeditation, but a plant which grew and ripened by degrees.

Hitherto John Wycliffe had only been known as a scholar and a college administrator. He was now to come forward in his second phase of a patriot and statesman ; but not yet, nor for many years subsequent, as a reformer of religion. In order to make his political proceedings clear, we must take a rapid glance over the history of the previous period—since that dark day in the annals of England when, to gain political help in an emergency, King John had laid himself and his kingdom prostrate at the feet of the Pope.

CHAPTER II.

THE ECCLESIASTICAL SITUATION. 1366.

HOSE persons who suppose that the Church of England began to exist at the Reformation, and that previous to that great dividing-point every Englishman was a member of the Church of Rome, show themselves lamentably ignorant of English history. No writer before the Reformation—even priests and friars included—ever saw the matter in that light. To them the Church of their country was always the Church of England, and the Church of Rome was an alien power, to be respected and treated with sisterly civility so long as she behaved properly, but to be resisted to the death as soon as she showed the slightest sign of arrogance or tyranny. The Pope was the pontiff of Western Christendom, who exercised as such certain legal and technical rights which must be submissively accorded, but who, when he stepped beyond those rights, was no more to be subserviently obeyed than a policeman is to be allowed to pick your pocket because he wears the uniform of a guardian of the peace.

It was on the 15th of May, 1213, that King John,

in order to obtain the Pope's help in his political
difficulties, both from within and without the kingdom, surrendered himself and England to the Pope,
receiving the latter again from the Pontiff as a fief
to be henceforth held of the See of Rome, by an oath
of fealty to the "successors of St. Peter," and the payment of an annual tribute of one thousand marks.
The words of Professor Lechler on this point are too
clear and weighty to be omitted.

"Thereby England became literally a member of
the Church-State, the King a vassal of the Pope,
and the Pope liege lord and sovereign of England.
England entered into and became a member of the
Papal State system, which already included Portugal,
Aragon, the kingdom of Sicily, Hungary, Bulgaria,
and other states—a relation to the Papacy which was
turned to practical account to the utmost of the
Church's power, by the levying of imposts from the
kingdom, as well as by the accumulation of English
Church offices and dignities in the hands of Italians.
But from the moment when King John made over
to the Papal See a feudal supremacy in England,
the moral influence of the Papacy in the country
began to stoop towards its overthrow. The English
nobility were the first to feel the humiliation most
deeply, and complained indignantly to the King that
he had brought what he had found a free kingdom
into bondage. . . . The King himself, in a letter to
Innocent III. (13th Sept. 1215), assures him that the
earls and barons of the kingdom publicly alleged
as the chief cause of their revolt his own act of

submission to the Pope ; and the Pope on his side considered the insurrection as directed in part against himself."[1]

On one point the Professor's words require a slight qualification. King John and Pope Innocent intended England to enter the Papal State system, but England herself, as we shall see more in future pages, sturdily and persistently declined to enter it. The Pope did his utmost to coerce her, and she bore it characteristically, grumbling and enduring, until at length, when the burden became too heavy for further carriage, she rose and shook herself free, having never in the interim ceased to protest against the imposition. But she never, knowingly and deliberately, laid herself down at the Pope's feet, a willing and subservient slave.

For one hundred and fifty years from that time, the ecclesiastical history of England may be likened to a wrestling-match between England and Rome. Rome poured into English ports a shoal of Italian priests, and England retorted by the constitutional steps of parliamentary debates and petitions to the Crown, and by the unconstitutional steps of plundering the possessions of the foreign ecclesiastics, keeping them in durance vile at the sweet pleasure of the populace, and mobbing the Pope's legate. Pope after pope appointed Italians to English sees and benefices, and king after king refused to confirm the appointments. Henry III., most inconsistent of men,

[1] Lechler's *John Wiclif and his English Precursors*, pp. 18, 19.

"constant to one thing, his inconstancy," admitted
the Italian priests when he wanted the Pope to do
something for him, and shut the door in their faces
when he did not. But Edward I. kept the door
systematically shut, forbade the introduction of Papal
Bulls into England, and hanged the Prior of St.
John for reading one to his monks. It was in his
reign, and by his cousin, Edmund Earl of Cornwall,
that the Predicant Friars were introduced into England. They were a branch of the Dominican Order,
and were then—not afterwards—so leavened with
the teaching of the *Boni-Homines*, or Waldensians
who were the Protestants of that period, that the
two Orders, of *Boni-Homines* and Predicant Friars,
were for all practical purposes identical. In fact,
the two principal religious houses founded by the
Earl—Ashridge and Edingdon—were of the Order
of *Boni-Homines*. During the reign of Edward II.,
this mixture of the Orders continued; and that
King, who may be termed our first Protestant king
from personal conviction, as distinguished from the
merely political anti-papal views of his father, through
the whole of his reign favoured the Predicant Friars,
and entrusted to them the education of his heir.
Of course those monks who had no sympathy with
his convictions gave him in their chronicles as bad
a character as they could. But the connection of
the Predicant Friars and the *Boni-Homines* came
to an end, at the latest, very early in the reign of
Edward III. He always retained a lingering affection for the Order, and for the teaching which he

had received from them; and the frequent flashes of anti-papal feeling and ecclesiastical independence which flit across his usually calm and impartial policy, are probably to be attributed to the foundation laid by the Predicant Friars.

By the time at which we have now arrived, the Predicant Friars had ceased to be preachers, and had become mendicants. They were now quite as bad as any of the other divisions. The four Orders of Mendicants—the Dominicans, Franciscans, Augustinians, and Carmelites—whose convents were richly endowed with the gifts constantly showered into their coffers, wandered up and down the kingdom, licensed beggars of the most objectionable kind, their morality being in many cases a minus quantity, and the laity nevertheless regarding them as holy persons, the least gift to whom would go to increase the donor's balance in the bank of Heaven. By a most ingenious fiction, the bare-faced impudence of which is really admirable (in the Latin sense of the word), all these richly-endowed Orders, with jewels by the score and pounds by the hundred in their coffers, had taken the vow of poverty, and were able with a clear conscience, as they understood conscientiousness, to declare themselves penniless and destitute. The Franciscans did so, because their property belonged to the Church; the Dominicans, because it pertained to the Order; the Conventuals (a variety of Franciscans), because they professed only to enjoy the interest of money, the property of which was still vested in the donors! Is there any length of absurdity to which a blinded intellect and a fettered conscience are unable to go? We shall see presently how, at a later period of his life, Wycliffe thundered against these men and their fraudulent "poverty." Those who look on monasteries as houses where the poor were helped and comforted, would do well to read his indignant denunciations of these "more than four thousand beggars," with their "sumptuous edifices, and superfluous expenditure," [1] who permeate the whole realm, "spoiling the kingdom" [2] and "spoiling the poor, teaching moreover that Christ thus begged," [3] which last statement in innumerable places he flatly writes down "a lie."

So early as the reign of Edward II., and only in his fourth year, certain brethren of St. Augustine had scandalized the Order by "wandering up and down the kingdom," and the King had issued commands for their arrest; [4] but the language used concerning these persons may perhaps indicate a condition of insubordinate demoralization rather than that of religious mendicancy.

Over and over again these Mendicants were "reformed," but a poor reformation it generally proved to be. The reformed Benedictines were known as Cluniacs, the reformed Cistercians as Gilbertines, the reformed Franciscans as Observants; but again

---

[1] *De Triplici Vinculo Amoris,* cap. ix., ed. Buddensieg, i. 193.
[2] *De Fundatione Sectarum,* cap. iv., *ib.,* i. 28.
[3] *De Ordinatione Fratrum,* cap. iv., *ib.,* i. 105.
[4] Patent Roll, 4 Edw. II., Part 2.

and again the reformed required reforming, until at last all the orders and divisions alike sank down into a vast seething mass of physical laziness and moral corruption. ,Individual exceptions no doubt there were here and there, and all honour be to those brave and God-fearing men who through all the moral mire around them kept their garments undefiled.

The natural result of this state of things was that the respectable and pious portion of society became disgusted with the Mendicant Orders, while to the disreputable portion they continued welcome. Men who desired to retain their sins while they avoided the punishment of them, found the constant giving of doles to these friars a very convenient way of fulfilling their religious duties ; and men whose vices were rather more numerous than they cared to have known, naturally preferred to confess them to an itinerant monk whom they might never meet again, rather than to the parish priest who had known them perhaps from childhood. As the Mendicant Orders descended in the scale of respectability, a new form of religious charity arose, which in Wycliffe's time was at the height of the fashion. This was the endowment of chantries where specially-appointed priests sang masses for the dead. That " new brooms sweep clean " is well known ; and so long as the chantries were a novel institution, the priests who served them appear to have been among the most respectable of their class. But apparently they did not long remain so.

The secular clergy, or parish priests, were not without their failings, nor are they left unsatirized by the great Reformer, who appears to have had as strong a dislike to a rich priest as Scott the commentator entertained to a wealthy Evangelical clergyman. The majority of them were bent on heaping treasure together and laying field to field, while the souls of their flock were left unshepherded. How, indeed, could the flock hope for any systematic feeding, when their pastor was frequently the holder of at least three or four livings, and only too often did not reside on the land at any of his cures? More than a hundred years before this, the upright soul of the evangelical Bishop Grosteste had been shocked at this perversion of righteousness, and he had done all that in him lay to secure a change. But as yet evil had been too strong for good, and the few endeavours of conscientious men to effect alterations had either fallen dead from their hands, or had dragged on but a faint life for a very little time.

Some of the best and most graphic pictures of those days have come down to us from the hand of a man who to some extent thought with Wycliffe, and can hardly be supposed not to have been his personal acquaintance. Indeed, the picture which he draws of a model priest is one for which many have supposed that John Wycliffe himself sat. Let us hear what Geoffrey Chaucer has to tell us of his Limitour, or mendicant friar licensed to beg within a certain district.

" A Frere there was, a wanton and a merry,
A Limitour, a full solempnè [1] man.
In all the Orders Four is none that can
So much of dalliance and fair language.
For he had power of confession,
As said himselfè, more than a curate,
For of his Order he was licentiate.
Full swetèly heard he confession,
And pleasant was his absolution.
He was an easy man to give penance,
There as he wist to have a good pittance; [2]
For unto a poor Order for to give
Is signè that a man is well yshrive. [3]
For if he gave, he durstè make avaunt,
He wistè that a man was repentant. [4]
For many a man so hard is of his heart
He may not weep although him sorè smart;
Therefore, insteadè of weeping and prayers,
Men might give silver to the poorè friars." [5]

It is necessary to enlarge upon this point, without
a good understanding of which much of Wycliffe's
life-work is unintelligible.

During the entire reign of Edward III., namely, for
thirty-eight years, the tribute laid upon England by
King John, to be paid to the Pope, had been in
abeyance. In 1365, Pope Urban V. sent to King
Edward, demanding the restitution of his tribute of
one thousand marks a year. There were further
offences than this, which had been offered him by

---

[1] Solemn.   [3] Shriven.
[2] Where he expected to receive a handsome present.
[4] Namely, if a man gave to a begging friar, the latter was
quite ready to pronounce him a true penitent.
[5] *Canterbury Tales*, prologue, lines 209—232.

England ; for Edward, like his grandfather, had no admiration for Papal Bulls, and had, six years before, imprisoned all persons who carried them in London ; nor did he permit the Pope to receive his fees from episcopal temporalities on the vacation of a see, except now and then when he had a point to gain.[1] Pope Urban, however, perhaps to show his affectionate forbearance towards his perverse English children, contented himself with only demanding his thousand marks. When this demand was made upon him, King Edward acted with the calm prudence which usually distinguished him, and which was more fully developed in himself than in any other of the Plantagenets. He called his Parliament together, on the 4th of May, 1366, at Westminster, and laying the question before them, he desired them to decide, in the name of the people of England, whether King John had any right thus to bind the nation, and whether if so the nation must then and ever continue so to be bound.

Let us picture to ourselves, bringing all our various details of information together, that Parliament whose decision was fraught with such momentous consequences for England. They sat, for the first day, in one grand assembly in Westminster Hall, after which they separated, the prelates going to the White Chamber, the Commons to the Painted Chamber. (The usual place for the Commons, however, was the Chapter House of the Abbey.) At the top of the "great hall" stood the throne, covered with red

---

[1] *Acta Regia*, p. 179 ; Lechler's *Wiclif*, p. 143.

embroidered in gold—the colours of England—and
on it sat the King—for a Plantagenet king was never
absent from the deliberations of his "great Council,"
either in person or by a solemnly-appointed deputy
—clad very probably either in a red robe covered
with golden lions, the arms of England, or in a blue
one powdered with golden lilies, the arms of France.
He would assuredly bear crown and sceptre, and
perhaps the orb as well.　On his right hand, ex-
tending far down the hall, sat the hierarchy, on this
occasion nineteen in number,—not as now in modest
black and white, but in robes of blue, red, lilac,
pink, and any other colour which it pleased them
to assume, always exhibiting a large white bosom,
probably an inner robe.　They were either bare-
headed, or wore a close warm hood.　Beneath them,
as we look down the hall, came twenty-three mitred
abbots, and below them two priors, and six masters
of arts, specially summoned by writ.　And there is
good reason to believe, though no writ of summons
remains on record, that among this last group sat the
Rector of Fillingham, John Wycliffe, who has written
sundry details concerning this Parliament which could
scarcely be the work of a man who was not present
at its deliberations.　It may also be indicated, as
Professor Lechler has suggested, by Wycliffe's description of himself as "the King's private priest,"
since no evidence is known to show that he was ever
a royal chaplain, the only alternative meaning which
appears probable.

On the left of the throne sat the peers, ten earls

and forty-one barons, not in any distinctive parliamentary robe—that was unknown in the Lollard
period, though it is found in the Tudor era—but in
the long robe, flowing to the feet, of any colour or
mixture of colours, girt about the hips, and probably
embroidered with some pattern in gold, or perhaps
plain and adorned with golden buttons; the sleeve
moderately tight, the stockings parti-coloured, the
shoes pointed, and the blue garter conspicuous below
the knee of such as were entitled to wear it. In the
presence of the sovereign, all heads would be bare;
the hair was worn of moderate length, and the beard
usually either forked or pointed. First of all, nearest
to the throne, would sit the King's son, John Duke of
Lancaster, then the premier Earl of England, Richard
Earl of Arundel and Surrey, followed by the rest of
the peers in due order; then came eight members of
the Privy Council summoned by writ, the knights
whose attendance the King had been pleased to command, by that act creating the individual a Baron of
Parliament—a dignity which did not descend to his
heirs—all the sheriffs except that of the Duchy, and
the Warden of the Cinque Ports. Lastly came the
"faithful Commons" (very unfaithful they sometimes
were)—the knights of the shire,—in those days the
majority of county members were really knights
—whom their constituents paid for their services
at the rate of four shillings a day, equivalent to
about three guineas and a half at the present value
of money; and the burgesses, or borough members,
who received half that sum. The sitting was expected

to last a much shorter time than now. For this
Parliament, two of the knights were summoned for
twenty-two days, and two of the burgesses for twenty.
The Lords sometimes sat longer than the Commons.

When the difficult question of the Papal tribute
was laid before Parliament, the bench of bishops
found itself in an awkward position, as might naturally be supposed. They asked for a day for private
consultation among themselves. When the great
Council re-assembled on the 5th of May, both spiritual
and temporal peers had resolved upon their policy.

The first who rose to speak, we are told, was " a
valiant soldier," but the names of the speakers are
not allowed to transpire. Wycliffe himself, in one of
his polemical tracts, is the reporter. Do we hear in
these plain words of the valiant soldier the voice of
the stormy-tempered, unscrupulous Arundel, of the
gallant warrior, Warwick, the stout Stafford, the
brilliant Suffolk, the uncertain Salisbury, or the
"faithful" Percy? It is tolerably sure to have been
one of the six.

" The kingdom of England," said this combatant
gentleman, " was of old conquered by the sword of
its nobles, and with the same sword has it ever been
defended against hostile attacks. And even so does
the matter stand in regard to the Church of Rome.
Therefore my counsel is, let this demand of the Pope
be absolutely refused, unless he is able to compel
payment by force. Should he attempt that, it will
be my business to withstand him in defence of our
right."

This doughty warrior having resumed his seat, the second peer rose. He said, "A tax or a tribute may only be paid to a person authorized to receive it; now the Pope has no authority to be the receiver of this payment, and therefore any such claim coming from him must be repudiated. For it is the duty of the Pope to be a prominent follower of Christ; but Christ refused to be a possessor of worldly dominion. The Pope, therefore, is bound to make the same refusal. As, therefore, we should hold the Pope to the observance of his holy duty, it follows that it is incumbent upon us to withstand him in his present demand."

The third peer spoke as follows :—"It seems to me that the ground upon which this demand is rested admits of being turned against the Pope; for as the Pope is 'the servant of the servants of God,' it follows that he should take no tribute from England except for services rendered. But now he builds up our land in no sense whatever, either spiritual or corporeal, but his whole aim is to turn its temporalities to his own personal use and that of his courtiers, while assisting the enemies of the country with gold and counsel. We must, therefore, as a matter of common prudence, refuse his demand. That pope and cardinals leave us without any help either in body or soul, is a fact which we know by experience well enough."

The fourth peer rose. "My mind is, that it is a duty we owe to our country to resist the Pope in this matter. For according to his principles, he is owner

D

in chief of all the property which is given to the Church, or alienated to her in mortmain. Now, as one third of the kingdom at least is so held in mortmain, the Pope is head over the whole of that third. But in the domain of civil lordship, there cannot be two lords of equal right, but there must be one lord paramount, and the other must be a vassal : from which it follows that during the vacancy of a church, either the Pope must be the vassal of the King of England, or *vice versâ.* But to make our King the inferior of any other man in this respect, we have no mind, for every donor in mortmain reserves to the King the right of feudal superiority. During that interval, therefore, the Pope behoves to be the inferior or vassal of the King : but the Pope has always neglected his duty as the King's vassal, and therefore by this neglect he has forfeited his right."

These were bold words. The fifth peer considered the question more at length. He inquired—

"What was the original ground upon which that undertaking was entered into?[1] Was that annual payment the condition of the King's absolution, and his reinstatement in the hereditary right to the crown? For a pure gift, and a mere beneficence for all coming times, it could not in any case have been. On the former supposition, the agreement was invalid, on account of the simony which was committed therein ; for it is not allowable to bestow a spiritual benefit in consideration of the promise of

[1] The concordat between King John and the Pope.

temporal gains to be bestowed. 'Freely ye have received, freely give.' If the Pope imposed the tax upon the King as a penitential penalty, he ought not to have applied this alms-gift to his own uses, but should have given it to the Church of England, which the King had wronged, as a compensation for the wrong. But it is not in accordance with the spirit of religion to say, I absolve thee, on condition that thou payest me so much in all time coming. When a man in this way breaks faith with Christ, other men may also break faith with him, in the matter of an immoral treaty. In all reason a punishment should fall on the guilty, not upon the innocent; but as' such an annual payment falls not upon the guilty king, but upon the poor innocent people, it bears more the character of avarice than of a wholesome penalty. If, on the other hand, the second case be supposed—that the Pope, in virtue of his concordat with King John, became feudal superior of the royal House, it would then logically follow that the Pope would have power, at his will and pleasure, to dethrone a king of England under pretext of having forfeited his throne rightly, and to appoint at his discretion a representative of his own person upon the throne. Is it not, then, our duty to resist principles like these?"

The sixth speaker followed in a similar strain.

"It appears to me that the act of the Pope admits of being turned against himself. For if the Pope made over England to our King as a feudal fief, and if, in so doing, he did not usurp a superiority which

D 2

did not belong to him, then the Pope, at the time of
that transaction with King John, was the lord of
our country.   But as it is not allowable to alienate
Church property without a corresponding compensation, the Pope had no power to alienate a kingdom
possessed of revenues so rich for an annual sum so
trifling : yea, he might at his pleasure demand our
country back again, under the pretence that the
Church had been defrauded of more than the fifth
part of the value.   It is necessary, therefore, to
oppose the first beginnings of this mischief.   Christ
Himself is the Lord Paramount, and the Pope is a
fallible man, who, in the event of his falling into
mortal sin, loses his lordship in the judgment of
theologians, and therefore cannot make good any
right to the possession of England.   It is enough,
therefore, that we hold our kingdom as of old,
immediately from Christ in fief, because He is the
Lord Paramount who alone and by Himself author-
izes, in a way absolutely sufficient, every right of
property allowed to created beings."

Perhaps the boldest note of all was struck by the
last speaker.   He said—"I cannot but greatly
wonder that you have not touched upon the over-
hastiness of the King (*i. e.* John), and upon the rights
of the kingdom.   And yet it stands fast that a hasty,
ill-considered treaty, brought on by the King's fault
without the country's consent, can never, with com-
petency and right, be allowed to operate to its
permanent mischief.   According to the custom of the
realm it is necessary, before a tax of this kind is

imposed, that every individual in the country, either directly or by his superior lord, should give his consent. Although the King and some few misguided persons gave their consent to the treaty, they had no warrant to do so, in the absence of the authority of the kingdom, and of the full number of consenting votes."

Truly, men spoke their minds freely in a Plantagenet Parliament! It was under the Tudors that their tongues were fettered, and they were told that unless they passed the King's Bill, he would have their heads off.

The vote was according to the speeches. The Parliament of England solemnly declared that

> "no Italian priest
> Should tithe or toll in their dominion;"

and that from that time forward, not one farthing of the thousand marks which he had claimed should be paid to the so-called successor of St. Peter.

The hierarchy, either from conviction or because they felt the stream too strong for resistance, voted with the lay peers.

The result of this action of Parliament was that a violent attack was made upon Wycliffe by an unknown monk, to which he returned answer in a pamphlet still extant, wherein he reports the speeches given above. This fact is almost conclusive evidence that Wycliffe was a member of the Parliament in question, if not by writ, then as one of the representatives of his archdeaconry; for two clerical delegates

from every archdeaconry were sent up to the council
of the nation : though the name he gives himself as
peculiaris Regis clericus seems rather to hint at a
summons by royal writ. Moreover, he must have
made his mark in some powerful speech (which he
has not reported), or why should he, the quiet Oxford
scholar, be singled out for special attack ? He seems
indeed tacitly to admit it himself, by saying, " Had I
spoken such things against my King, they would have
been inquired into before now, in the Parliament of
English peers." Surely not, unless the speaker were
himself a member of that Parliament !

The tumult of 1366 died down, and the Pope did
not then reassert his claims. Wycliffe himself subsided into his previous calm student life, pursuing his
literary labours, and discharging such of his parochial
duties as he found compatible with other calls. But
the world did not forget the powerful statesman of
whom it had caught a glimpse behind the scholar :
and when next the question required handling,
England looked to the Rector of Ludgershall, and
found him ready to answer.

CHAPTER III.

NE of the many abuses which had been growing in the kingdom during the previous ages was that the clergy had gradually drawn into their hands nearly all the offices of state. The Lord Chancellor, the " keeper of the King's conscience," had been a priest from time immemorial : the Treasurer, the Lord Privy Seal, and many members of the Privy Council, were now priests likewise. In 1371, the Parliament, which had in the interim been growing more and more anti-clerical, proposed to the King that all these offices should be in future filled by laymen, who would be amenable to the civil courts if they committed any offence. Shortly after this, in February, 1372, the Pope sent over as his nuncio a French canon named Arnaud Garnier, empowering him to collect all Papal dues in this country. This worthy gentleman was not particularly welcome to any body in England, except to that section of the public which found it convenient to " compound for sins they were inclined to " by pecuniary payments to those

agents of the Church or the Pope facetiously termed
" spiritual men." The nuncio remained in England
for two years and a half, and then carried his spoils to
Rome, with the intention of presently returning to
pick up any further golden eggs which might be
obtainable from the Anglican goose. But before his
return, in 1373, Parliament urged the King to resist
the constant and annoying interference by the Pope
with the rights of English patrons. King Edward
upon this sent to Avignon, July 20, 1373, a commission, consisting of John Gilbert, Bishop of Bangor, Sir
William de Burton, Friar Ughtred of Durham, and
Master John de Shepeye, to lay the matter before
the Pope's delegates at Avignon, and endeavour to
extract a promise of better behaviour for the future.
The Pope gave them conciliatory words, but prudently
refrained from any distinct promise. Instead of the
latter, he once more despatched Canon Garnier to
pick up anything worth bringing away.

When the Papal receiver had originally come to
England, the King had demanded of him a solemn
oath to the effect that he would in his official
proceedings defer to the interests of the Crown and
kingdom. Nevertheless, he had carried out of the
kingdom a heavy sum in gold, which was thereby
lost to the Church of England. The King resolved
on another embassage to the Roman See, and he was
determined that this time it should be sufficiently
powerful and imposing. The commissioners named
were John Gilbert, Bishop of Bangor (head of the
former commission), " our beloved and faithful Master

John de Wiclyf, S. T. P.," Master John Guteri,[1] Dean of Segovia, Master Simon de Multon, Doctor of Laws, Sir William de Burton, Roger Bealknap, and John de Honyngton.[2] The commission warrant styled these persons the King's " ambassadors and procurators," and they were instructed to proceed to " foreign parts, for the purpose of treating and consulting benignly and charitably with the nuncios and ambassadors of the Lord High Pontiff concerning the said negotiations for which we formerly sent " the Bishop of Bangor and his colleagues ; "and to make a full report to us and to our Council of such matters treated and consulted between them, so that those things which can conduce to the honour of holy Church and the security of our Crown and of our kingdom of England may be happily forwarded in that respect by the providence of God and of the Apostolic Chair, and they may receive the debt in full."

This looks rather as if the bold speeches of his

[1] So spelt on the Close Roll, 48 Edw. III., Part I., from which Professor Lechler conjectures him to be an Englishman appointed to the deanery of Segovia ; but seeing that he appears in the Register of John of Gaunt as Gittiers and Guttiers, in a compotus of that Prince as Gultiers, in his own compotus as Guterry, and that another John Guttiers in the Duke's household, named De Camargo to distinguish him from the Dean, is expressly termed a Spaniard, I think there can be no doubt that his real name was Juan Gutierrez.

[2] Close Roll, 48 Edw. III., Part I. The last name is certainly Honyngton, not Kenyngton, as given by some modern writers. His compotus, which styles him Doctor of Laws, also gives the name as Honyngton.

peers had somewhat failed to satisfy King Edward himself, so that he was prepared to consider the Papal tribute as a just debt. This commission was issued on the 26th of July, 1374, and on the very next day the embassy set sail from London for Bruges, where they were to meet the Pope's commissioners. The Public Record Office contains a bundle of small documents relating the sums of money paid to each member of this embassy, and the dates of his departure and return. From the "Particulars of the Account of Master John de Wyclyf, S.T.P., concerning his journeys and expenses, going on the King's embassy to Flanders, for the King's business,"[1] it appears that sixty pounds were paid "into his own hands" at the Exchequer, from the Treasurer and Chamberlain, on the 31st of July. This certainly seems to contradict the assertion that he set out on the 27th of July, which the same document goes on to state. He was absent fifty days, returning on the 14th of September; which at the rate of one pound a day, the King's allowance to him, added to 42s. 3d., the cost of his voyage to and fro, comes to £52 2s. 3d. He had therefore received above the sum spent, £7 17s. 9d., for which he would have to account to the Treasury.

The allowance was extremely handsome, being equal to £18 a day in the present time : but Edward III., while he was no spendthrift, always paid hand-

---

[1] Queen's Remembrancer's Office, 48 Edw. III., Miscellaneous, Nuncii, 630/48. Quoted Addit. MS. 24, 511, fol. 124.

somely. The allowance made to the Duke of
Lancaster on his embassies was £5 a day. The
Bishop of Bangor had £3 6s. 8d., and the Dean of
Segovia £1 per day.[1]

At the same time and place, a treaty was pending
between England and France, and the ecclesiastical
commission found already at Bruges the political
ambassadors—John of Gaunt, Duke of Lancaster,
William de Montacute, Earl of Salisbury, and Bishop
Sudbury of London. The embassy sent by the
Pope was equally imposing. The Archbishop of
Ravenna and the Bishop of Carpentras were com-
missioned to watch the political negotiations; while
the Bishops of Pampeluna and Sinigaglia, and the
Provost of Valencia, were appointed to treat of the
ecclesiastical questions. The persons selected seem
to show good-will on the part of the Pontiff, since
the two Spanish dignitaries were subjects of John
of Gaunt as *de jure* King of Castilla, and the Bishop
of Carpentras appears to have been his personal
friend.[2]

It was not improbably through the influence of
the Duke of Lancaster that Wycliffe was appointed
on this embassy. He and Chaucer were both personally known to this Prince, and the latter was about
this time a member of his household. Wycliffe's
views, at least politically, were shared by the Duke

---

[1] Queen's Remembrancer's Office, 48 Edw. III., Nuncii,
Calendar.

[2] A gift of plate to him, probably on New Year's day, is
recorded in the Duke's Register for 1372.

all his life; the spiritual portion of his teaching was not so welcome at the Savoy Palace.

During Wycliffe's sojourn in Bruges, he had the opportunity of becoming acquainted with the feelings and opinions of many persons whose influence in the Roman Church was of a powerful character. It has been generally supposed until lately that it was at Rome that these negotiations were conducted, and that the effect produced on the mind of the Reformer by his sojourn in the "holy" city was exactly the same as that conveyed a hundred and fifty years later to the mind of Martin Luther. The place was a mistake; Wycliffe never was at Rome in his life. But the result produced on the two reformers was true enough. The meeting between Wycliffe and the Papal commissaries not only strengthened his spirit of resistance to Papal claims, but, so far as evidence leads us to judge, produced in him, or at least confirmed, those germs of suspicion and mistrust of the truth of Roman doctrine which never appear to have troubled him until about this time, but which after this grew and developed, slowly at first, more rapidly afterwards, until they led him to stand out as the great champion of infant Protestantism, and to characterize him who was termed Christ's Vicar as above all others the adversary of Christ.

It has been the custom of modern writers on Wycliffe to assert that Edward III. sent him on an embassy to Milan—of which his best biographer, Professor Lechler, makes no mention, nor is any

trace to be found among the ambassadorial com-
potuses. There is, however, a small and partly
illegible scrap of parchment among the Queen's
Remembrancer's official documents,[1] from which
it appears that "Master John de" *something* was
sent to Flanders, by Dover and Calais, leaving
London on May 1st, and returning on the 30th.
£10 15s. 4d. were paid him for the expenses of his
journey, and he was accompanied by a man-servant
and a horse. The year is uncertain, but the probable
figure is "anno 28"—namely, 1354. It is possible
that this may have been Wycliffe. The surname
is absolutely illegible, only a part of the first letter
remaining, which looks like the beginning of either
B or W.

On the first of September Pope Gregory presented
his ultimatum to the English Government, couched
in a series of Bulls. His Holiness was evidently
not devoid of worldly wisdom. The spirit of the
whole transaction on his side may be summed up
in the homely words—"Don't say anything about
it, and I won't do it again!" Accomplished facts
were to be recognized by England, and for the
future Rome would no longer attempt to challenge
royal appointments or the rights of patronage in
England. But King Edward, on his part, was
required to abstain from conferring dignities without the Pope's sanction : a condition which largely
nullified the concession just made. The important
point of the rights of Cathedral Chapters, which

[1] Miscellanea, Nuncii, 630/17.

Parliament had urged strongly, was passed over in discreet silence; and not a word was spoken to indicate that the Pope might not, at some future time, again demand his tribute of a thousand marks.

Eleven days after the issue of these bulls, the Pope nominated the Bishop of Bangor to the See of Hereford. The head of the commission had evidently lost nothing in the eyes of the Roman See by his conduct in this transaction. How far he had fulfilled his duty to king or country it might not be out of place to inquire.

The ecclesiastical congress appears to have sat longer than the political one, for the Duke of Lancaster was at Leicester Castle as early as the 1st of August. Wycliffe retired once more into private life; but he did not return either to his hired rooms in Queen's College, or to the Rectory of Ludgershall. His final promotion had been conferred upon him a few weeks before he left England for Bruges. On the 7th of April, 1374, King Edward conferred on his " private priest " the Rectory of Lutterworth, in the county of Leicester, seven miles from Rugby. Thither John Wycliffe went, probably glad to rest, and not sorry to have a quiet time granted him, within which to revolve all the new and strange ideas which his recent experiences had awakened within his brain.

Henceforth the name of the place is inseparably associated with that of the Reformer, and the one glory of Lutterworth is Wycliffe. It is a small market town, situated on a gentle rise in the midst

of a flat district, consisting of rich pasture land.
It rejoiced in a river (the Swift), a petrifying spring,
a cage for the detention of evil-doers, a cucking-
stool for scolds, and a parish cat-o'-nine-tails. We
may not unreasonably deduce from these properties
a conclusion that Lutterworth must have been kept
in exceptionably good behaviour by all these means
of correction—unless we are to suppose the deplorable
opposite, that it must have been very bad to require
so many of them !

The church of Lutterworth is the same edifice in
which Wycliffe ministered, though the aisles had
only been added about thirty years before he became
its Rector. It was built at the close of the thirteenth
century, and originally possessed a spire, blown
down in a storm in 1703. Over the chancel arch
is a curious mediæval fresco of the Day of Judgment.
The upper portion of the pulpit is believed to be as
old as Wycliffe, and the communion chair is tra-
ditionally the one used by him ; there is also an oak
table preserved in the church, at which he is said to
have fed his poor parishioners. Experts have, alas !
declared chair and table too modern for authenticity.
The font of Wycliffe's day is in the Museum at
Leicester, and the church itself has twice undergone
the generally cruel and Vandalic process termed
restoration—a process by which the visible history of
the hapless building is swept away previous to an uncertain date, and it is turned into what the nineteenth
century supposes it to have been before whatever
period it may be pleased to select. Whether the

twentieth century will be thankful to its immediate predecessor for these labours is—well, I should think, *not* doubtful.

The benefice of Lutterworth, though conferred on Wycliffe by King Edward, was only in his gift through an accidental lapse to the Crown. The manor and advowson belonged to the ancient family of Ferrars of Groby, and it was because the then Lord Ferrars was a minor that the presentation was for the moment vested in the King. Henry Lord Ferrars, a youth of seventeen, possessed a wife and a stepmother; and these two excellent ladies were just at that time engaged in a very " pretty little quarrel " concerning the manor of Lutterworth. The stepmother, Lady Margaret Percy, who was aunt of the Earl of Northumberland, claimed the manor as a portion of her dower lands; while the wife, Joan Poynings, who was probably older by some years than her very youthful husband, asserted that her husband had endowed her with the manor; and each lady strenuously maintained her personal right. The Lady Margaret urged that young Henry had no power to enfeof any person with the manor; and the King seems to have thought her in the right, for he commands justice to be done to her,[1] according to the law and custom of England.

In the following year, Wycliffe was created Prebendary of Aust; but he appears to have resigned it almost at once, for in the November following, Robert de Farrington was appointed to the office.

---

[1] Close Roll, 48 Edw. III., Part .

The quiet rest at Lutterworth had been merely a period of repose in which to prepare for action. The Rector was called once more to the front, and when this time he took up shield and spear, it was that he might never lay them down again till he should rest in the Paradise of God.

Ever since the Spanish campaign—namely, for some eight years past—the Prince of Wales, commonly known later as the Black Prince, had been in very weak health, suffering from a complication of disorders contracted in Spain. He felt death drawing near, and he became anxious on a point in respect of which his father also felt with him—the question of the succession. Edward III. was now, as men went in his day, a very old man. His son, in the flower of his age, appeared likely to die before him, and his son was a little child of nine years old. Modern writers are naturally puzzled to know why the Prince felt any doubt of the peaceful succession of this boy, and are driven to a hypothesis of the ambitious temper of John of Gaunt, the younger brother of the Prince. This ambition of John of Gaunt is shown by all evidence to be so completely imaginary, that it is surprising more should not have doubted the truth of this solution of the puzzle. The real explanation lies in an entirely different quarter, and it has been overlooked because it never entered any one's head that there could be any solution of the kind. As Wycliffe seems to have taken an active part in the matter, and to have had a decided opinion on the question, we shall not be travelling out of the record,

L

to use a legal phrase, in examining the point at issue.

This point at issue was the simple fact that the young son of the Prince had no right to succeed. Because he would have had it now, historical writers have strangely neglected to inquire how far it was the case then. He had it not, being shut out by "the custom of England," which strenuously denied representation, or the right of a grandson to step into the place of his deceased father while his grandfather was alive, or into the inheritance at his death. The real heir was John of Gaunt, the very man of whose ambition so much has been made; and had he in reality been ambitious, the matter would have ended very differently from the way it did. Had he wished to be king of England, he not only could but would have been so, by the simple expedient of holding his peace—namely, of refusing, if the expression may be allowed, to cut off the entail in his own favour.

How, then, was the change made? By Act of Parliament, influenced by the wills of the old King Edward and the dying Prince, and assisted by the readiness of the true heir to assent to the arrangement, and by the extreme dislike with which he was regarded by the citizens of London. The reasons of this unpopularity are more difficult to fathom. The Duke of Lancaster was a man whose faults lay much on the surface. He was hot-tempered, like all the Plantagenets; he cared very little what people thought of his actions; he was not a man of pure moral life, though by no means so bad as some modern writers

would make him out to have been; he possessed
great administrative powers, and he enjoyed exercising them. But what he enjoyed more than anything else was taking his ease. His feats, whether of
war or statecraft, were mostly performed in pushes.
Let his fitful energy die out, and his physical and
mental activity be overcome by his moral inertia, and
he was ready enough to go home and lie on the sofa.

The Prince of Wales, though a better general than
his brother, was by no means so good a statesman.
The exact nature of his short-sighted desire to
see his son upon the throne cannot be ascertained
with any certainty. But this we know, that he belonged to the orthodox party who wished to retain
religion *in statu quo,* and his Princess and the Duke
of Lancaster sided with the active party who called
loudly for a reform in the Church. That there were
no priestly wire-pullers all through it is not possible
to believe, though in this instance they managed to
keep their cards much better concealed for a time
than upon some subsequent occasions.

The end of all these intrigues was the assembling
of what was afterwards known as the Good Parliament, at Westminster, on the 28th of April, 1376.
On the side of the Prince were the House of Commons, and the clergy, who now came forward and
exhibited themselves. They brought solemn accusations of malpractices and dishonesty against the
Treasurer, Lord Latimer, and the Lady Alice Periers,
—both personal friends of the Duke of Lancaster,
and let it be especially noted, prominent members

E 2

of the Lollard party. And a few more lines must be added concerning these two persons, in order to make matters clear.

Thomas Lord Latimer of Braybroke appears in John of Gaunt's Register as the recipient of gifts from the Duke, and they were evidently on terms of intimate friendship. It was he who, twenty years later, in company with Sir Richard Stury, even a stronger Lollard than himself, took the bold step of presenting to Parliament the Lollard manifesto termed Sir John Oldcastle's Book of Conclusions ; and he was one of the four members of the royal household who were rebuked for their "heretical" proclivities by King Richard in 1395, when for a short time that monarch's eyes had been blindfolded by the subtleties of Archbishop Arundel. His wife was in attendance on the Princess of Wales, and was rewarded by a grant of £20 per annum for bringing news to the Prince of the birth of his son Richard. The terms of his will have been supposed to prove that he died "a great penitent," in other words, that he recanted his Lollard views. It is difficult to see any evidence of this in the will itself, couched in language of the most abject humility—a grace which surely is not restricted to those who are not Protestants—unless it be supposed to lie in a single line,—" Therefore I pray to [God] meekly of His grace, that He will take so poor a present as my wretched soul is into His mercy, *through the beseeching of His blessed mother and His holy saints*"—and this is no more than many a Lollard would have written. The invocation of saints was one of those articles in respect to which some went much further than others. If the fragment entitled " Ave Maria" ascribed to Wycliffe be genuine, he was not when he wrote it free from that error.

Concerning Alice Periers more must be said, since there are some errors rife about her which need refutation. The popular notion concerning her is that she was originally a maid of honour to Queen Philippa, to whom, after the death of her mistress, Edward III. transferred the affection which he had previously restricted to his wife, suffered her to govern him at her pleasure, held a tournament in which she figured as " Lady of the Sun," and bestowed upon her the entire wardrobe and jewels of the dead Queen. Let us look first at the three concluding points, and we shall then be better able to judge of the second. The story of the tournament comes from Stow, who does not give his authority for it, and it may be true or false. If true, I fail to see what it proves, except that the woman selected for such a position was most likely to be beautiful. Alice Periers never was a maid of honour : she was lady of the bedchamber to Queen Philippa, as is attested by many entries of her name upon the Rolls, where she is always termed *domicella cameræ*, and never *domicella Reginæ*. Therefore, as the ladies of the bedchamber were *ipso facto* married women, it follows that Periers was her married name, and not, as has always been supposed, her maiden name. The gift of the wardrobe and jewels, of which so much has been made by her enemies, who are not dead yet, turns out on examination of the original grant to be a gift of "all jewels, goods, and chattels, which were ours and our deceased consort's, and were sometime in the hands of Euphemia de Heselarton, and were received by the said Alice from the said Euphemia for our use."[1] Surely there is a distinction between "all my goods" and "all my goods in a certain place"; nor can any reasonable being believe that King Edward would, if in his sober senses, bestow every atom of his property upon Alice Periers or anybody else, or that if he were otherwise, his council would have permitted the grant to take effect.

With respect to the moral charge against King Edward, no less than against Alice, I own to a feeling of astonishment that any one who has studied his character, not to speak of hers, can possibly believe it. During sixty-three years he had led a life of moral purity to which in his immoral age it would not be easy to find a second. And is it to be imagined that such a man, at the age of sixty-three, would suddenly alter so totally and so much for the worse as this accusation presupposes? Let those credit it who can. I cannot; nor could Dr. Barnes, the historian of Edward's reign; nor Mr. Carte, the most careful and accurate of historical writers. The strong probability is that the King, towards the close of his long life—in the eyes of his contemporaries it was a life of marvellous length—fell into a condition of

---

[1] Patent Roll, 47 Edw. III., Part II. This is the real donation, so far as it exists : the entry more commonly quoted is merely an indemnity to Euphemia for delivering the jewels to Alice, without written warrant.

imbecility, marked it may be with lucid intervals. Many little circumstances point to this conclusion, and it is the more likely, since it is even a greater certainty that the same thing, for a much longer time, was the case with his mother. Now, if this were so, as there is every cause to believe, and as some of the most judicious writers on the period have thought probable, it became necessary that some woman, of discreet years and good judgment, should be placed in personal care of the imbecile old man. Etiquette would prevent this position being assigned to his daughter, the Princess Isabel, who moreover, there is reason to think, was in very delicate health, and certainly was suffering under acute mental agony through the desertion of her husband. A lady would naturally be chosen to whose face and voice the King was accustomed, and Alice Periers had been in the Queen's service for three years at least, so that he must have been perfectly familiar with her as one of those constantly about him. This position of nurse and care-taker is exactly the position in which we find Alice. The charges brought against her were that she admitted or refused admittance to persons who came to speak with the King—the very duty of a nurse ; and as we find that the King was in bed on these occasions, it seems evident that he was ill : that she sat at the head of the King's bed when he gave audiences, and that she spoke to him in private when others were not admitted to do so. All this points to the sick nurse, whose duty it was to watch the old man perpetually, and to put an end to any interview which she might think too long or exciting for the strength of her patient. The tournament, if there were one, may have been got up for the purpose of amusing the King, or perhaps at his desire, persisted in with the warmth and obstinacy of a mind off its balance, and his physicians might consider it unwise to thwart him.

This hypothesis is the more probable, since the accusations against Alice's moral character are found only in one class of writings. They spring entirely from the chronicles written under the influence of Henry IV., with the express purpose of blackening the characters of those who had a hand in changing the law of succession. The genuine charges brought against her in Parliament comprised no hint of this kind. They had to do merely with the exercise of influence over the old King, relative to incidents entirely of a political character, and especially concerning a certain Nicholas Dagworth, who was at enmity with Alice's husband, Sir William de Windsor.

I have been more particular in detailing these points, because the circumstances, which are in close connection with Wycliffe's life, are generally much misunderstood. Even Foxe, misled by the monkish chroniclers, formed a mistaken view of the character and history of Alice Periers.

Of course the person really aimed at in all these charges, but too high to be distinctly included, was the Duke of Lancaster. That the charges were false, is sufficiently shown by the fact that the next Parliament spontaneously requested the revocation of the sentence. Very severe were the penalties inflicted. Alice Periers was banished from England; but though forced to retire from Court (probably to the detriment of her royal charge), she exhibited her spirit and her sense of innocence by declining to quit the country, and merely going to reside at a distance from town with her second husband, Sir William de Windsor, one of the doughtiest warriors of the campaigns of Edward III.

The Good Parliament (whose proceedings were not unmixed with evil) proceeded to alter the succession to the throne. The little Prince Richard was introduced to the House on the 25th of June, and was solemnly recognized as the successor of King Edward ; the first person to take the oath of future allegiance being his uncle of Lancaster, who thereby divested himself of his legal rights. If he could also have divested his son Henry, who followed him, of his ambitious spirit and desire of revenge, the following reign would have been much less tempest-uous than it was. For Henry never forgave any person who had a share in that act, and his own father least of all.

One of those present was the Rector of Lutterworth. That he sat in the Good Parliament, probably by royal summons, is more certain than that he occupied a similar place in that of 1366. And that his vote was against the alteration of the succession is probable, and that it was against the persecution of his friends is more than probable. The Duke

of Lancaster would scarcely have taken so prominent
a part in favour of Wycliffe in the ensuing February,
if Wycliffe had joined the plot against him in the
previous June.

But before the sitting had progressed far, and
before the change in the law of succession was
assured, Edward Prince of Wales, the darling of
the English people, had no more a portion in the
things that are done under the sun. He died in his
father's Palace of Westminster, on Trinity Sunday,
the 8th of June, 1376; so much at variance with his
Lollard Princess that he is said to have refused the
farewell interview which she entreated. This statement, however, rests upon rather suspicious authority;
but the fact that the husband and wife were not on
good terms appears true enough.

His last words have been preserved to us.

" Blessed Trinity, whose name I have always
worshipped on earth, whose honour I have laboured
to increase, in the faith of whom, though otherwise
a wretch and a sinner, I have ever lived, I pray Thee
that as I have magnified this Thy feast in earth,
and have called the people to do Thee honour and to
rejoice with me in this Thy feast, Thou wilt deliver
me from this body of death, and count me worthy to
partake that most delightful festival which is being
celebrated to Thy glory this day in Heaven." [1]

Wycliffe himself has recorded the Prince's character as " of orthodox affection towards the Trinity,

---

[1] *Chronicon Angliæ*, quoted note to Wycliffe's tract *De
Demonio Meridiano*, Latin Works, ii. 417.

and defender of the Trinitarian faith in this realm." [1]
But he was not kindly affected towards that infant
Reformation which was soon to become the dearest
thing upon earth to the Rector of Lutterworth.

The work of the Good Parliament—it was the
citizens of London who so dubbed it—was not by
any means finished when it had ensured the change
in the succession. A yet more important part of
its business consisted in the ecclesiastical grievances
which it brought under the royal notice. The King
was desired to take special note of six points.

(1) The aggressions of the Pope are the cause
of the impoverishment of the realm, for the official
dues of the See of Rome amount to five times as
much as the Crown taxes.

(2) The decay of learning in the kingdom is due
to the iniquitous action of the Church brokers, who
promote men of bad character and no scholarship
to the wealthy livings for the sake of filthy lucre.

(3) The service of God is brought into contempt
by foreigners, and even enemies, possessing these
livings, and never going near their parishioners to
fulfil the duties incumbent on such possession. "God
has entrusted the care of the sheep to the Pope, to
feed them, not to fleece them."

(4) The Papal Receiver, a spy and a Frenchman,
"has a great house in London, with clerks and
offices, as if it were the custom-house of a prince,
and thence he sends to the Pope about twenty
thousand marks a year." He has also this year put

---

[1] *De Demonio Meridiano*, Latin Works, ii. 417.

forward a claim to firstfruits. Let no receiver or agent henceforth take up his residence in England, upon pain of losing life and limb ; nor shall any Englishman become such an agent to persons who reside in Rome. Let John Strensale, priest of St. Botolph's, who has been for five years clerk to the Receiver, be examined on this head.

(5) Cardinals and other foreign prelates, some natives of England, but most of them residents in Rome, are in possession of the best prebends in England. The Deans of York, Salisbury, and Lincoln, and the Archdeacons of Canterbury, Durham, and Suffolk, are all foreign cardinals. When a bishopric is vacant, the Pope translates from four to five bishops from place to place in order to possess himself of the firstfruits of each see ; and he claims the right of election to all abbeys and convents, which have hitherto enjoyed the right of free election.

(6) The Pope raises subsidies from the English clergy for the purposes of ransoming French prisoners, and carrying on wars in Lombardy ; " in addition to which the English clergy are required to bear the cost of every mission which the Pope sends to the country, and all this is done purely out of love to the kingdom and to English gold."

Parliament also reminded the aged monarch that this was his year of jubilee, and he could accord no greater grace to his land than to redress these grievances.

The old dying man to whom these energetic

remonstrances were addressed gave but a languid answer. The time was past when his hand had been firm upon the sceptre, and his voice as clear in its strength and independence as the utterances of his Parliament. Now the orb was dropping from his hand, and he had chosen that it should pass into the weak inexperienced hand of a little child, instead of into that of a man in the prime of life, who was one of the ablest administrators of the century. Was he "very wise, or very foolish"? The event would show.

CHAPTER IV.

WYCLIFFE'S FIRST TRIAL. 1377.

EFORE the sitting of the Good Parliament was closed, the first note had been sounded on that tocsin of persecution which was ever after to dog the steps of John Wycliffe. He was speaking—doubtless against the Papal usurpations—when Thomas Trillek, Bishop of Rochester, sprang to his feet with that ominous word which was to be appended to the Reformer's name thenceforward. Doubtless in most Parliamentary language, he desired to remind the Hon. Member that his theses had received condemnation as heretical from the See of Rome. It was the first word which the world had heard of the sentence, to come forth only in the following May by Papal Bull : it may have been the first word which Wycliffe had heard himself.

The matter was not suffered to rest by the hierarchy. As the Bull was not yet issued, no actual process for heresy could be undertaken ; but some occasion must be found against this unbearable Daniel. What they did at last find by way of accusation is a matter involved in considerable obscurity, except that it was of a political rather than a religious nature : but who the man was that found it is not left in obscurity. It was the first step taken by Bishop Courtenay on a road which he afterwards traversed to the bitter end.

On the death of Archbishop Langham, in 1375, the Bishop of London, Simon Sudbury, was chosen to fill the primacy. He was a quiet, mild, unenergetic man. The Bishop of Hereford succeeded him in the See of London. And we must give a little study to this new Bishop of London, for he exercised no inconsiderable influence on the remainder of Wycliffe's life, and on what might otherwise have been the result of Wycliffe's labours. To him and to one other man is due the wretched distinction of having stifled the English Reformation at its Lollard birth. Their assistants, whether priests or statesmen, were merely their obedient servants.

William Courtenay, Bishop of London, and in the course of a few years Archbishop of Canterbury, was a younger son of the numerous family of Hugh, first Earl of Devon, and the Lady Margaret de Bohun, a granddaughter of Edward I. He was therefore the second cousin of the King, and was a man of some five-and-forty years of age. A portrait almost certain to be his [1] is extant in the beautiful little MS. known as King Richard's Prayerbook,[2] and it shows us a man with fair hair and

[1] There is only one other whose likeness it can be, Alexander Neville, Archbishop of York.
[2] Cott. MS. Domitian, A. xvii, fol. 176.

surprised eyebrows. That he was an extremely clever, subtle, worldly-wise man, no one can doubt who studies his actions. The one point of his character which deteriorated from his wisdom was that he was a violent man. He was not one who knew how to wait, and he occasionally injured his own cause by over-precipitancy. For all this, he contrived, during an episcopacy of four years, and a primacy of sixteen, to do about as much mischief to the Church of England as a clever, violent, unscrupulous man could well do. This was the man who, with all the power of the first bishop in England, now entered the lists against the Rector of Lutterworth.

In order to secure the change in the Act of Succession, and to shut out the Duke of Lancaster, of whom they were sorely afraid, it pleased the clergy to spread abroad a silly tale to the effect that the Duke was not the son of King Edward. They asserted that Queen Philippa had on her deathbed confessed to Bishop William de Wykeham that her real child was not a son, but a daughter, whom she accidentally smothered in sleep, and fearing the King's wrath when he should return from England, procured a substitute in the child of a poor woman at Ghent, who was now known as the Duke of Lancaster. The whole tale was a tissue of improbabilities, not to say impossibilities, made all the more unlikely by the facts that the Duke had the true Plantagenet character, and in face was about as like his father as he could be. It may be sur-

mised that the Duke himself would not particularly
admire this sensational anecdote, nor feel any special
emotion of affection or gratitude to the class who
were diligently spreading it.

But there was no cause for surprise that the clergy
should have taken alarm, for the Court of the dying
King was filled with Lollards, and it was tolerably
certain that the Court of his successor would be even
more so. Lord Latimer, the Treasurer, Alice Periers,
and John de Salesbury, squire of the chamber, were
among the prominent members of the body. Sir
Simon Burley, tutor of the young Prince Richard, Sir
Lewis Clifford, squire of the body to the Princess of
Wales, Lady Anne Latimer, of her bed-chamber, and
John Worth, seneschal of her lands, were in the same
position. The Confessor of the Duke of Lancaster,
Walter Disse, was a pronounced member of that
party. The Archbishop of York was, to say the
least, kindly affected towards them, while his brother,
Sir William Neville, was considered the chief of
the party ; and their sister was that Euphemia de
Hesclarton who had been Queen Philippa's jewel-
keeper.

There can be little doubt that had it been in their
power, the clerical party would have chosen some
other person than Prince Richard to supersede the
obnoxious Duke of Lancaster. His mother, the
Princess, who had great influence over him, was
completely committed to the "new doctrines," and
she was no woman of soft or undecided character, but
one possessed of great energy and strong will. It is

F

not improbable that at this juncture she exercised
some pressure on the Duke of Lancaster, which
caused him to take the decided steps he did. For
shortly after the Good Parliament rose, the Duke laid
a firm hand upon the reins of power. The clerical
party, suddenly and much to their astonishment,
found themselves transported from the top of the
wheel of fortune to the bottom. Sir Peter de la
Marc, the Speaker, who had taken the chief place in
the plot against the Duke, was accommodated with
somewhat restricted lodgings in Nottingham Castle ;
Lord Latimer received a pardon ; and Alice Periers,
Lady Windsor, returned to Court, in calm contempt
for the sentence of banishment inflicted on her by the
clerical caucus. Had John of Gaunt only gone on
as he began, all might have been well. For a time
things were well. And having thus for the moment
settled the political crisis, the Duke began to turn his
attention to ecclesiastical affairs, in pursuit of which
purpose he sent to Lutterworth for his friend John
Wycliffe.

When the bishops heard that their great enemy
had arrived at the Savoy Palace, they were frightened
indeed. Something must be done ! The Lollard
Duke was sufficiently formidable as head of the
State ; but if he began to meddle with the Church,
who could tell to what lengths he might go ? They
rushed to Lambeth in great agitation, and worried
the gentle Archbishop Sudbury until at last he con-
sented to issue a citation to the Rector of Lutterworth
to appear before Convocation in the Lady Chapel

of St. Paul's Cathedral, on the 19th of February
following.

Meanwhile King Edward grew weaker and more
incapable every day. Richard Prince of Wales was
appointed honorary viceroy of the kingdom ; no un-
usual thing for a mere baby at that time. He had
been chosen to preside at the sitting of the next
Parliament, and the royal warrant expressly enjoins
him to fulfil the duty in person. But the real ruler
was John of Gaunt, one of whose fitful bursts of
energy had come upon him, and behind whom stood
probably the Princess of Wales, and certainly the
Rector of Lutterworth.

" For the moment," writes Professor Lechler, " the
prelates were no match for the Duke in the political
arena ; but all the more readily on this account they
seized the opportunity of indirectly humbling him in
the ecclesiastical province, in the person of a theo-
logian who stood in intimate relations to his person." [1]

On the 27th of January, 1377, the little Prince
of Wales opened Parliament at Westminster ; and
on the 3rd of February Convocation met in the
Lady Chapel. The 19th arrived, and the Rector of
Lutterworth made his appearance before a body of
judges predetermined to condemn him if they could
find any possible loophole through which to do it.
" Here, then, stood Wiclif before his judges, awaiting
his examination—a tall, thin figure, covered with a
long, light gown of black colour, with a girdle about
his body ; the head, adorned with a full, flowing

[1] Lechler's *Wiclif,* p. 183.

F 2

beard, exhibiting features keen and sharply cut ; the eye clear and penetrating ; the lips firmly closed in token of resolution—the whole man wearing an aspect of lofty earnestness, and replete with dignity and character."[1]

But the Reformer did not appear before his enemies alone. By his side came Henry Percy, Marshal of England, and beyond him the virtual king, the Duke of Lancaster himself. The two great enemies and cousins faced each other—Lancaster and Courtenay —the blood of the Plantagenets throbbing in the veins of both, and both, at that moment, equally vindictive and equally determined. Alas, that the man who was in the right was so sadly infirm of purpose, while the man who was in the wrong held on his way unfaltering !

Behind them came a band of armed men, and four or five mendicant friars, whom the Duke had summoned to his aid in favour of Wycliffe—one of the confirmatory proofs that Wycliffe's fervent opposition to the mendicant orders had scarcely begun at this date. Several friends of the Reformer also attended him. This mixed suite of the Prince and the Professor found it hard work to push through the Cathedral, and to reach the Lady Chapel at the further end. There was of course some noise and disturbance accompanying their appearance : in connection with which Bishop Courtenay soon showed the spirit in which he had come thither.

"Had I wist," said he, addressing Lord Percy,

---

[1] Lechler's *Wiclif,* p. 184.

"·the fashion wherein you went about to play the master, within this house of God, then would I have debarred you of entering therein."

The reply was quite as peppery as the remark which had called it forth, but it came from the Duke of Lancaster.

"*I* will be master here, though ye all say nay!" was the regal answer of John of Gaunt.

As soon as Wycliffe had reached the bar of the tribunal, Lord Percy desired him to sit down.

"You have need to rest yourself, for you will have many questions to answer."

Up sprang the Bishop of London in towering wrath.

"He shall not sit! Neither is it lawful nor becoming that one cited to answer before his ordinary should sit during the time of his answer. Let him stand."

A violent quarrel ensued between the Marshal and the Bishop. Percy, however, was a better hand at cajolery than abuse; and he was soon and thoroughly overmatched by Courtenay, whose capacity for railing appears to have been among his most brilliant qualities. Seeing the Marshal borne to earth in the tournament of words, the Duke came to his aid; but Courtenay proved more than a match for him also. John of Gaunt could make hasty speeches in the heat of his anger, but to descend to vulgar quarrelling as the Bishop was doing was beneath the son of King Edward. He stopped, blushed, and then said sternly—

"I will bring down the pride, not only of thee, but of all the prelacy of England! Thou bearest thyself so brag upon thy parents, who shall not be able to help thee : they shall have enough to do to help themselves."

When this threat reached him—which was likely to be no idle one, considering the source whence it came —Courtenay suddenly became very meek and pious.

"If I may be bold to tell truth," he answered, "my affiance is not in my kinsmen, nor in any other but in God, in whom alone I put my trust."

The Duke was not capable of passing from fire to ice with the crafty versatility of his episcopal relative. Once more he flared up in red-hot anger.

"I will sooner pluck that caitiff out of the church by the hair of his head, than I will put up with such an affront at his hand!" were the words of John of Gaunt, addressed in a low voice to that member of his suite who stood nearest. But unfortunately the voice was not low enough. It was overheard by several citizens of London standing in the vicinity, and they immediately added their sweet voices to the already sufficient tumult. They took the Duke's threat very literally.

"Never will we suffer our Bishop to be thus shamefully handled!" they cried. "We will rather lose our lives than see him dragged forth by the hair!"

During all this time Archbishop Sudbury sat still in his chair, and Wycliffe stood quietly at the bar, neither having uttered a word. But now, doubtless thinking that the brawling had lasted long enough, and was likely to lead to worse rather than better, the Archbishop interposed, and wisely dissolved the sitting, at nine o'clock in the morning. The Duke, the Marshal, and the Professor withdrew with their friends, the matter was at an end, and the citizens of London were left to get cool again as best they might. The Duke and Lord Percy went at once to Parliament, where they took vengeance on the City. That very morning the King's youngest son, the Lord Thomas of Woodstock, a young man only just of age, rose and moved, and Lord Percy seconded, a motion that the government of the City should no longer be in the hands of the Lord Mayor, but should be submitted to a captain as in time past, proposing the Lord Latimer for that post. The Marshal was also to be at liberty to arrest criminals within the boundaries of the City.

It is likely that when this young Prince thus rose on the side of his brother and the anti-clerical party, the Lollards then present in Parliament congratulated themselves and thanked God on the promise of his youth. If they could have looked a few years forward, they would have beheld this promising youth develope into the very cruellest and wiliest of all their lay persecutors, second only to Bishop Courtenay and his colleague and successor, Arundel.

When the news of this motion came forth to the London world—communicated doubtless by John Philpot, Member for the City, who with many "words of stoutness" had opposed the motion—it was as fuel to the fire of wrath raging among the citizens. A complete riot followed. First they rushed to St. Martin's Lane, where they stormed Lord Percy's house ; and, disappointed in not finding him at home, they next dashed through the streets to the Savoy Palace, where they hoped to find him with the Duke of Lancaster. Happily for himself the Duke also was absent, for he and Lord Percy were at that moment eating oysters in the house of John de Ypres, one of the richest of the Flemish merchants settled in London. The Duke was a very good customer of this John de Ypres, who had been seneschal of King Edward's household, and whom entries in his Register show that John of Gaunt treated as a personal friend. One of the Duke's servants got away quietly from the besieged palace, and came running to Knight Riders' Street to tell his master of the insurrection. The Duke, with his usual precipitancy, sprang up in a hurry, "breaking both his shins at the form for haste," and, followed by Lord Percy, took boat and rushed off to the Princess, a strong indication that she had been his principal adviser. It is the only time in his life that John of Gaunt is known to have conducted himself like a man thoroughly frightened. The Princess and the young Prince were at Kennington Palace, then one of the quietest and most rural spots in the vicinity of London. She did not lose her head as her brother-in-law had done.

"Leave it to me," said the Princess, calmly. "I will take such order in the matter as shall content you."

While the Duke was thus running away to Ken-

nington, the citizens were stormily deliberating the
pulling-down of the Savoy Palace. News was brought
to Bishop Courtenay, as he sat at dinner, that if somebody did not interfere, the incensed crowd would
probably take this form of revenge upon the Duke.
Whereupon this peaceful prelate assumed the aspect
of a turtle-dove, and came to his wolfish flock at
the Savoy.

"My brethren," said he, with a tongue steeped in
honey, "have you forgotten that this is the blessed
season of Lent? Cease, then, from strife, and go
quietly home, like good Catholic Christians."

He had, a few hours previously, most pointedly
forgotten it himself ; but perhaps he was of opinion
that

> "That in the captain's but a choleric word,
> Which in the soldier is flat blasphemy,"

and thought a bishop so sanctifying a person that
passions which were sins in the crowd of Londoners
were but venial imperfections in him. The crowd,
awaking to the realization that they had already
murdered an unhappy priest, who had offended them
by speaking in uncomplimentary terms of Sir Peter
de la Mare, and recognizing that the Church might
be rather awkward to deal with in consequence, dis-
persed in comparative quiet, only amusing themselves
on the way by half killing one of the Duke's gentlemen who was so unfortunate as to meet them, and
reversing the arms of that Prince wherever they came
across them. Since the heraldic signification of this
action was to declare their opinion that the Duke

was a traitor and worthy to be hanged, it may be supposed that the proceeding would not be considered flattering on his part.

How the Princess mediated between the citizens and the King, and the Duke and they were reconciled, are matters which belong to general history. We have to do with John Wycliffe, thus delivered from the mouth of the lion at the moment when that angry beast had rushed upon him with open jaws. The riot had ended a long way from him and his opinions. It is not even known where he was while all these transactions were taking place. Perhaps he was among the guests of John de Ypres; but very shortly afterwards he was probably journeying home to Lutterworth, there to remain until the enmity of the prelates should summon him away from his pastoral work again.

For nearly a year they suffered him to rest. He seems to have spent it quietly at home in ministering to the spiritual needs of his parishioners. And here we must revert to that portrait of a minister of Christ, drawn by the hand of his friend Geoffrey Chaucer, and drawn, as has been often surmised, from the model of John Wycliffe.

> "A good man there was of religion
> That was a poorè parson of a town,
> But rich he was of holy thought and work.
> He was also a learned man, a clerk,
> That Christès gospel truely woldè [1] preach ;
> His parishens [2] devoutly would he teach.
> Benign he was, and wonder [3] diligent,

---

[1] Would.   [2] Parishioners.   [3] Wondrously.

And in adversity full patient ;
And such he was yproved often sithes.[1]
Full loth were him to cursen for his tithes,
But rather would he yeven [2] out of doubt,
Unto his poorè parishens about,
Of his offering, and eke [3] of his substance.
He could in little things have suffisance.[4]
Wide was his parish, and houses far asunder,
But he ne left nought for no rain ne thunder,
In sickness and in mischief [5] to visite
The furthest in his parish, much and lite,[6]
Upon his feet, and in his hand a staff.
This noble ensample to his sheep he yaf,[7]
That first he wrought, and afterward he taught.
Out of the Gospel he the wordès caught,
And this figure he added yet thereto,—
That if gold rustè, what should iron do ?
For if a priest be foul, on whom we trust,
No wonder is a lewed man [8] to rust : . .
Well ought a priest ensample for to give
By his cleannessè, how his sheep should live.
He settè not his benefice to hire,
And let his sheep acumbered [9] in the mire,
And ran unto London, unto Saint Poules,
To seeken him a chanterie [10] for souls,
Or with a brotherhood to be withhold ; [11]
But dwelt at home, and keptè well his fold,
So that the wolf ne made it not miscarry.
He was a shepherd and no mercenary.
And though he holy were and virtuous,
He was to sinful men not dispitous,[12]
Ne of his speechè dangerous ne dignè,[13]
But in his teaching discreet and benign.

---

[1] Since. [2] Give. [3] Also.
[4] Sufficient. [5] Accident. [6] High and low.
[7] Gave. [8] Layman. [9] Encumbered, stuck fast.
[10] Chantry : there were thirty-five in St. Paul's Cathedral.
[11] Retained. [12] Contemptuous, unpitying. [13] Prou 1.

To drawen folk to Heaven with fairèness
By good ensample, was his business :
But it were [1] any person obstinate,
What so he were of high or low estate,
Him would he snibben [2] sharply for the nonce.[3]
A better priest I trow that nowhere none is.
He waited after no pomp ne reverence,
Ne maked him no spiced conscience [4];
But Christès lore,[5] and His Apostles' twelve,
He taught, but first he followed it himselve." [6]

We may see plainly from this sketch not only
what sort of man Wycliffe himself was, but also the
common faults of the clergy in his day, for avoiding
which the poet gives him praise.

It is now time to inquire what those theses were
which Wycliffe had been drawing up, and which the
Court of Rome had been so hasty in its anxiety to
condemn. With respect to all reformers, and to
Wycliffe among them, it is at once important and
difficult to draw a sharp line of demarcation between
what their enemies asserted that they said, and what
it can be proved that they really did say. Some of
the assertions made at a later period as to Wycliffe's
views—we shall come to them presently—are of a
nature which no unbiassed judgment can seriously
believe him to have held. But the nineteen theses
condemned by Pope Gregory's Bulls, Wycliffe himself acknowledged, and offered explanations of them
at his second examination. They were as follows :

---

[1] But if it were.   [2] Rebuke.   [3] Occasion.
[4] This very likely means, he did not attempt to disguise the
truth in order to make himself agreeable.
[5] Doctrine.   [6] Himself.

I. "The whole human race concurring, without Christ, have not power absolutely to ordain that Peter and all his meynie should rule over the world politically for ever.

II. "God cannot give civil dominion to any man for himself and his heirs for ever.

III. "Many charters of human invention, concerning perpetual civil inheritance, are impossible.

IV. "Every one being in justifying grace not only hath a right to all the things of God, but hath them in possession.

V. "A man can give dominion to his own or his adopted son only ministerially, whether that dominion be temporal or eternal.

VI. "If God be, temporal lords can lawfully and meritoriously take away property from a delinquent Church.

VII. "It is not possible that the Vicar of Christ, merely by his Bulls, or by them with his own will and consent and that of his college of cardinals, can qualify or disqualify any man.

VIII. "It is not possible that a man should be excommunicated to his damage, unless he be excommunicated first and principally by himself.

IX. "Nobody ought to excommunicate, suspend, or interdict any, or proceed to punish according to ecclesiastical censure, except in the cause of God.

X. "Cursing or excommunication does not bind, except in so far as it is used against an adversary of the law of Christ.

XI. "There is no power granted by Christ to His

disciples of excommunicating a subject for denying temporalities, but the contrary.

XII. "The disciples of Christ have no power co-actively to exact temporalities by censure.

XIII. "It is not possible by the absolute power of God that if the Pope or any other Christian pretend that he bindeth or looseth as he will, he does, therefore, actually bind or loose.

XIV. "We ought to believe that the Vicar of Christ either binds or looses, only when he obeys the law of Christ.

XV. "Every priest rightly ordained, according to the law of grace, hath a power according to which he may minister all the sacraments, and by consequence may absolve any contrite person confessing to him from any sin.

XVI. "It is lawful for kings, in cases limited by law, to take away the temporalities from clergy who habitually abuse them.

XVII. "If the Pope, or temporal lords, or any other person, have endowed the Church with temporalities, it is lawful for them to take them away in certain cases: namely, when the act is by way of medicine to cure or prevent certain sins; and that notwith-standing excommunication or any other Church censure, since these endowments were not given but under a condition implied.

XVIII. "An ecclesiastic, even the Roman Pontiff himself, may lawfully be rebuked by his subjects for the benefit of the Church, and may be impleaded by both clergy and laity."

The nineteenth article is not given by Foxe, but Professor Lechler, who does not repeat the theses, states it to be a mere amplification of the one preceding it.

These theses are not by any means easy to understand. They are here copied chiefly from the translation of Lewis, but simplified so as to be more intelligible to modern readers. But however they may be simplified, it would in some cases be hard to comprehend the meaning of the Reformer if we had not the light of his own explanation of them. His German editor, Dr. Rudolph Buddensieg, remarks that Wycliffe's Latin is particularly obscure, not only from his constant use of English idioms, but from his long paragraphs and involved construction.

One point will naturally strike the reader—that these theses are, one allusion in Article XV. excepted, entirely outside the region both of faith and practice. They relate only to questions of legal right or ecclesiastical discipline. And as there can be no doubt that the hierarchy, who so diligently sought for some cause against the Rector of Lutterworth, would have gladly availed themselves of any expressions which they could twist into heresy in matters of faith, we may reasonably conclude from their silence that at this time they were unable to seize any such occasion.

On the 22nd of May, 1377, Gregory XI. issued his five Bulls in answer to the appeal of the English hierarchy against John Wycliffe. The first three, addressed to the Archbishop and the Bishop of London, command them to ascertain by private inquiry whether these propositions have been actually put forth by John Wycliffe; if so, they are to commit him to prison, to report proceedings to the Pope, and to await his further instructions. If Wycliffe, obtaining intelligence of what is intended, should endeavour to save himself by flight, the prelates are endowed with full power to issue a citation binding him to appear in person before the Pope at Rome within three months from the date thereof. Lastly, they are to bring these wicked propositions before King Edward and his sons, the Princess, and other great persons and privy councillors, and to point out to them the dangers threatened to the State. The fourth Bull, addressed to the King, informed him of these facts, and besought his aid and protection for the prelates in the discharge of their duty. The last, addressed to the Chancellor and University of Oxford, required them, upon pain of the loss of their privileges, to guard against all erroneous doctrine, to commit Wycliffe and his obstinate followers to prison, and to deliver them to the prelates above-mentioned. The whole power of England and of Rome was convoked against this one man. But greater was He that was with him than all that were with them.

Before any steps had been taken by the prelates in consequence of these Bulls, the long weary time of weakness and imbecility was over in Shene Palace, and the longest reign then ever known in England had an end. King Edward died on the 21st of June, 1377, nursed by Alice Periers devotedly to

the last—for which her enemies rewarded her by
diligently spreading a calumny that she had deserted
him in his last moments, after stripping the rings
from his powerless fingers. Rarely has monarch been
mourned so truly or so deservedly as he. He had
held a just balance, and had kept a pure Court ; he
had ruled his people with a golden sceptre, ready
to pardon where he could see just cause, yet not
letting criminals loose upon society from weakness
of purpose or morbid sentimentality ; forbearing to
wring imposts from his subjects to minister to his
own pleasure or splendour, but keeping up the state
and honour of England in the eyes of foreign powers.
Gentle and just had been his rule for fifty years,
and his people sorrowed for their loss. Could they
have looked forward and have foreseen the deluge
which was to come after him, the sorrow might have
been bitterer yet.

The nominal ruler of England was now that fair-
haired, beautiful boy of ten years old, whom the
deceased Prince and the citizens of London had
chosen to be his successor. The real rulers were
the boy's mother and uncle, Joan Princess of Wales,
and John Duke of Lancaster. A third, of whom
nobody had thought, was biding his time—that clever,
subtle, astute young Prince, afterwards to be known
as Thomas Duke of Gloucester, who had stood
forward against Bishop Courtenay and the citizens
six months before. And in the background, hidden
in the shadows, yet concealed most of all by the
mask of their own smiling faces, stood those two yet

more astute priests, Courtenay and Arundel, ready
to wait any time and to endure any hardship,
content so that only their victim should not escape
them. The nets were being drawn round the Rector
of Lutterworth. Would there be any hope of
escape ?

CHAPTER V.

WYCLIFFE'S SECOND TRIAL AND THE GREAT SCHISM. 1377—1381.

THE solemn funeral of the dead King in Westminster Abbey, and the splendours and festivities attending the coronation of his successor, were only just over, when the episcopal and other enemies of the Lollard party began to gather their forces together for a second persecution. Political perils also threatened the new rulers in no small measure. There was a heaving and seething movement among the Commons, in the double sense of the House and the populace. The former went so far as to put forward a claim that in future the appointment of all officers of State should rest with itself: a suggestion which, it may be imagined, was regarded as preposterous by the Lords. On the Papal question, moreover, the House of Commons was so outspoken, that the hierarchy thought it prudent to await the prorogation of Parliament before they showed the rod which they held concealed. This took place on the 25th of November, 1377 ; and on the 18th of the following month, Courtenay struck the blow for which he had been forced to wait so long.

But not even Courtenay dared to act upon the stringent terms of the Pope's Bull. In the episcopal mandate to the University of Oxford, commanding the Chancellor to ascertain, with the aid of "learned and orthodox doctors of Holy Scripture," whether John Wycliffe were really the author of the theses put forward in his name, there is not the faintest hint of imprisonment. The Chancellor is merely ordered to report the result to the Archbishop, and to cite Wycliffe to appear within thirty days before the Papal commissioners or their deputies in St. Paul's Cathedral. The commissioners had good reason to be cautious. In the first place, the fidelity of the University to the Papal cause was more than uncertain; and in the second, Wycliffe was just then in the highest favour at Court. The House of Commons had struck a blow direct at the Roman appointments by petitioning that from the 2nd of January, 1378, all foreigners, whether monks or seculars, should be forced to depart the kingdom, and that all property belonging to such persons throughout the country should be confiscated for the purposes of the French campaign. "The income of French clergy alone, accruing from English livings, was estimated at £60,000 a year."[1] The question had also been proposed and warmly discussed in Parliament, "Whether the kingdom of England, in case of need, for the purposes of self-defence, is not competent in law to restrain the treasure of the land from being carried off to foreign parts, although the Pope should demand

---

[1] Lechler's *Wiclif*, p. 193.

this export of gold, in virtue of the obedience due to him, and under the threat of Church censures." [1]

The council of the young King—which really means, the Princess of Wales and the Duke of Lancaster—wishing to have an opinion upon this important question, applied to a learned doctor to give them one; but not, in the view of the hierarchy, an orthodox doctor. Instead of appealing to the bench of bishops, who, being "spiritual persons"—though some of them knew little what manner of spirit they were of—were in their own eyes the proper people to decide any question of this kind, they actually sent for that identical John Wycliffe against whom no less than five Papal Bulls were outstanding at that very moment. Could anything have been imagined better calculated to increase the flame of Courtenay's wrath ?

Wycliffe, ready when called upon, drew up the opinion demanded. He puts the question through three sieves—the law of nature, the law of Scripture, and the law of conscience ; and upon every count he returns an affirmative answer. Every corporate body, according to the first law, possesses the power of resistance for self-defence : all almsgiving (which is the source of Church property), according to the second, ceases to be a duty in case of necessity of the donor. The argument from the third law is not preserved.

But, terrible as this act of Wycliffe was in the eyes of Courtenay, it was not nearly equal in gravity to another offence which he had committed. During

[1] Lechler's *Wiclif*, p. 193.

that quiet year at Lutterworth, 1377, the "old hypocrite"—this is the clerical party's favourite epithet
for the Reformer—had been presuming to take into
consideration the current state of affairs with regard
to preaching.   It was more than time that somebody
should give some attention to the subject.   Before the
original institution of the Predicant Friars, preaching
had fallen into complete desuetude.   By them the
practice had been revived, and sermons were much
more usual in the fourteenth century than in the
twelfth or thirteenth.   But very odd discourses many
of them were.   The best were those of a logical and
intellectual type, and only the more respectable members of the priesthood preached even these.   The
commoner style of sermon was replete with songs,
jokes, and laughable anecdotes, sometimes descending
even to scandalous stories, which in the present day
would be deemed unfit for publication.[1]   The exceptions in which anything was preached which bore
even a distant resemblance to the Gospel of Jesus
Christ were as few and far between as angels' visits.
Wycliffe set to work to improve this state of things.
He established a school of the prophets, wherein he
trained young men, and sent them forth as itinerant
preachers, giving special attention to those two
counties—Oxfordshire and Leicestershire—with which
he was himself particularly connected.

Courtenay's wrath burnt fiercely against this pre-
sumptuous man at Lutterworth.   What business had

he to set himself up to reform preaching throughout England, when my Lords the Bishops had not stirred in the matter? Wycliffe, on his part, looked at the question in the light of severe simplicity and common sense. The thing wanted doing; somebody must do it; and the persons whose duty it was did not do it. The matter, therefore, fell naturally into the hands of any one who chose to take up the neglected duty. This was a light in which the episcopal defaulters could not be expected to see it. In their eyes, right was on the side on which they chose to be; if they did not attend to anything, it could only be because no attention was necessary, and no one had any business to question so obvious a fact.

As certain troublesome formalities had to be gone through before Wycliffe could be legally attacked, the clerical party turned its attention for the moment to the business of disposing of the smaller Lollards. A fresh charge of exercising undue influence over the deceased King was brought against Alice Periers, and in this instance her enemies were more powerful than before, being reinforced by the Duke of Lancaster, who appears to have quarrelled with his former friend, and who himself gave evidence against her. Alice was banished again, and again declining to accept the sentence, she retired into private life. John of Gaunt's Lollardism, at all times merely political, always gave way before his private interest, and during the latter half of 1377 he seems to have been in a very bad temper. There certainly is some excuse for him, since the ugly reports which the clerical party had been industriously spreading had come to his ears, and he was evidently extremely hurt and angered by them. He went so far as to defend himself against them in Parliament, saying that "if any man charged him with disloyalty, he was as ready to defend himself with his body as the poorest bachelor amongst them." Hierarchy, Lords, and Commons rose as one man, and utterly repudiated any hand in the reports, or any belief in them. The Duke then said he was ready to forgive the past, but his indignant words show that he had felt it deeply. He withdrew from Court, promising to return if the King needed his help, and leaving matters in the hands of the twelve peers and knights who had been chosen with him to conduct public business, and—unostensibly—in those of the Princess of Wales, who contrived at that time to be at the bottom of everything. Thus Wycliffe lost his protector, who, like a sulky bear, went off growling to Kenilworth, and left matters to conduct themselves as best they might. And—ominous fact!—among the twelve notables thus chosen to govern the kingdom, the gentle Archbishop Sudbury, and the Lollard Archbishop Neville, did not appear; but they counted in their ranks the two chief persecutors, Bishop Courtenay of London, and Bishop Arundel of Ely. Wycliffe might well have trembled, if he had not believed in his God.

The commissioners soon found that their suspicion of the fidelity of Oxford to the Papal cause was fully justified. The University "hesitated long " whether to obey the Papal Bull addressed to themselves. They did, however, obey the archiepiscopal mandate, and cited Wycliffe to appear before the commissioners.

The gentlemen last named, meanwhile, were pleased to pour forth their own praises from brazen trumpets of no small size. They publicly declared that no entreaties, threats, nor bribes, should be allowed to influence them for an instant in this matter—not even if their own lives should be the forfeit. (As nobody wanted their lives in the slightest degree, they were quite safe in saying so.) They would bend neither to prince nor peer, till they had punished the arch-heretic ![1]

No such words came from Lutterworth. The Reformer knew better than to waste his strength in blowing bubbles like these.

These " glorious boasters " (the term is that of their faithful servant, Walsingham) took their seats at Lambeth—whither they had for some unknown reason adjourned : it is likely, to avoid evoking the Wycliffite citizens of London—on the 30th of January, 1378, and once more Wycliffe placed himself at their bar. He handed in a paper wherein he firmly but modestly defended his theses, first protesting "as I have often before done, that I purpose and will with my whole heart, by the grace of God, to be an entire Christian, and as long as breath shall remain in me, to profess and defend the law of Christ, so far as I am able. And if, through ignorance or any other cause, I shall fail therein, I ask pardon of my

[1] In all this, Courtenay was really the responsible person, as Sudbury merely followed meekly in his train.

God, and do now, as before, revoke and retract it, humbly submitting myself to the correction of holy mother Church. And forasmuch as an opinion concerning the faith which I have taught in the schools and elsewhere hath been reported by children,[1] and moreover hath been conveyed beyond sea by these children, even to the Court of Rome, therefore, lest Christians should be scandalized on my account, I wish to set down in writing my opinion, for the which I am impeached, the which opinion I will defend even unto death, as I believe all Christians ought to do, but specially the Bishop of Rome and the rest of the priests of the Church. But I understand the conclusions after the sense and manner of speaking of the Scripture and the holy doctors, the which I am ready to expound; and if the conclusions shall then be found contrary to the faith, I am willing and most ready to revoke them." [2]

The protest now proceeds to explain the nineteen theses given in the last chapter. The explanation

---

[1] We should now say, "young people."

[2] Foxe, *Acts and Monuments*, III. 13, 14. It has been the fashion lately in some literary circles to sneer at Foxe as a credulous old simpleton, who allowed himself to be imposed upon to any extent so long as the imposition chimed in with his preconceived views. It is a little singular that only High Church writers are able to discover these deplorable blunders of Foxe; and that all unbiassed persons who inquire into the question (including in this case the German writers upon Wycliffe) find Foxe's documents wonderfully valuable and accurate, and that his suggestions on doubtful points frequently come nearer the truth (when discovered) than those of later writers.

is long, and would not perhaps be deemed generally
interesting : I shall therefore confine myself to
noticing such points of it as interpret the more
obscure passages, or such as might be wrongly
understood without them.

I. He explained that by "ruling over the world
politically " he meant civil, or secular government,
all which must have an end at the coming of Christ,
and could not therefore last for ever.

VI. On the curious clause, " if God be," he reasons
thus :—If God be, He is almighty : if so, He can
command temporal lords to take away the property
of a delinquent Church : therefore, they may lawfully
take it away. "But God forbid that from thence it
should be believed . . that secular lords can lawfully
take 'it away when and howsoever they please, or
by their bare authority; but they may do it only
by the authority of the Church, and in cases and
form limited by law."

XII. His gloss upon this is Luke xxii. 25, 26.
" The kings of the Gentiles exercise lordship over
them . . but ye shall not be so."

In conclusion, he said,—" God forbid that truth
should be condemned by the Church of Christ,
because it soundeth ill in the ears of sinners and
ignorant persons : for then the whole faith of the
Scripture would be liable to be condemned."

The protestation was given in, the commissioners
were about to give sentence, those troublesome
citizens of London, who had cruelly followed the
poor prelates to Lambeth—" yea, even the abjects

of the city," growls Walsingham—had interposed in vain with intercessions. Suddenly there was a little stir at the door, and the prelates looked uneasily in front of them to see if they were once more to be balked of the game which they had taken so much pains to run down. Poor things! they were again doomed to disappointment; and as if to make their misfortune even more humiliating than on the previous occasion, they were baffled by a woman. What they saw was Sir Lewis Clifford, himself a Lollard, and knight of the body to the Princess of Wales. He came forward coolly, and announced himself as the bearer of a message from his royal lady. In right royal language it was couched.

The Princess of Wales forbade the Council to proceed any further, "or to presume to pronounce anything in the form of a sentence against the said John."

Poor Bishop Courtenay! how terribly irritating to him must have been that irreverent word, *presume!* One of the sheep opened its mouth, and sharply rebuked the shepherd for his arrogance! A woman desired a bishop not to presume! He swallowed the impertinence—with how wry a face is not on record. But he knew he could go no further—*then.* The roaring lion suddenly subsided into the cushat-dove—the angry shepherd became meek as a lamb. The Council was dissolved—Wycliffe was dismissed uncensured.

Woful was the disappointment, and terrible the wrath, of the clerical party. "One would have

supposed that their mitres had lost their horns!"
shrieks the Popish chronicler, Walsingham, who seems
almost beside himself with rage, at this lame and
impotent conclusion of a matter begun so exultingly.
" The crafty hypocrite had the better of his judges,
and got clean off."

We may feel pretty sure that prayers went up
for the Princess Joan, and benedictions were pronounced on her that night in many places. And we
may be even surer of one place—the Bishop of
London's Palace—where something was allowed to
fall on her head which was not at all likely to be
a benediction.

John Wycliffe turned away from Lambeth on that
morning, a true and faithful son of what he then
understood as the Church Catholic. He might,
humanly speaking, have remained so, but for one
historical event, which dashed the dust from his eyes,
and showed him in the figure that he had hitherto
seen imperfectly, not the pure bride of Christ, but
the woman of the Seven Hills, with the golden cup of
abominations in her hand. On the 27th of March,
1378, two months after the abortive trial at Lambeth,
Pope Gregory, the persecutor of Wycliffe, passed to
his account ; and then began that great Schism of the
West which was the event destined to open the eyes
of John Wycliffe to the real character of that Church
which he had hitherto deemed the very fountain of
purity and truth.

Cardinal Bartolomeo Prignano, Archbishop of
Bari, who took the name of Urban VI., was elected

in the room of the deceased Pope Gregory. He proved after a time so proud a man, and so harsh a ruler, that his subjects speedily rebelled, and on the 20th of September, 1378, elected Count Robert de Genève in his stead, who assumed the title of Clement VII., and was the first Antipope. Urban issued a violent Bull against his adversary, on the 29th of November; and a bloody war, not only metaphorical but literal, began between the rival Popes. England, Germany, Portugal, the Scandinavian kingdoms, and Flanders, sided with the original Pope, Urban; Scotland, France, Spain, Savoy, and Sicily, espoused the cause of the Antipope, Clement.

Urban VI. had begun his reign so well, that he had given great hopes to the Lollards of a reformation of many abuses under his auspices. Wycliffe, in his early polemical tracts, speaks of him personally with great respect. At a later period, when his opinion of the man's character had changed, he still speaks with deference of the Pope; but at the close of his life, all respect either for man or office has departed, and he can only behold, whether in pope, in antipope, or in papacy, the great enemy of Christ.

The great Schism of the West shocked all thoughtful minds to a degree which it is perhaps difficult for a modern Protestant to realize. For Christendom to have two popes was to them as unheard-of and preposterous as for a man to have two heads. It was the scandal of scandals—beyond anything ever imagined. And it was not a mere item of foreign news, to be discussed and dismissed, as it would be now, but a question which came home to every man's conscience and life. An opinion must be formed, and a choice made, and a policy determined on. Political feelings were also brought into play, for Clement was in every sense the French Pope, and to support Urban against him became a point affecting the national honour of England.

The practical effect of all this upon Wycliffe was to make him more earnest in sending forth his itinerant preachers, and to evoke from him the first of those polemical writings which beyond anything else help us to trace the growth of his opinions. In 1379 he issued that which was not improbably the first of the long series—the treatise headed, "The Two Kinds of Heretics."

These two kinds he defines as Simonists—namely, popes, bishops, and curates, who are guilty of Simony ; and Apostates—priests, especially prelates, who have lost the true faith. According to the Scriptures, lepers are to dwell apart. All heretics are spiritual lepers. Therefore, they ought to be driven out, "and with them their abettors, the clergy, mendicant friars, and temporal lords who support them. They can, indeed, only be expelled by a miracle, for the whole world is full of them." [1]

Henceforward Wycliffe comes before the world in

---

[1] *Polemical Works, Wyclif Society,* ii. 429. The polemical tracts can be more or less dated ; to the English sermons it is impossible to affix any chronology. The latter must therefore be treated of by themselves.

his fourth and last character of a voluminous author.
Tract after tract pours forth from his pen, some in
English, some in Latin : sermon after sermon is
found, some very likely preached to his own flock at
Lutterworth, but more apparently intended for the
use of his itinerant preachers. But he also now
began a more important work than either—the
translation of the Bible.

Before Wycliffe's day, there had been translations
of various parts of Scripture into Middle English—
that is, the language spoken in England from the
Conquest to the Reformation. The Psalter had been
translated more than once ; but no English version of
the whole Bible had been attempted, much less
accomplished. This priceless boon John Wycliffe
gave to the English people—first the New Testament,
and then the Old. His version was necessarily made
from the Vulgate, the only form in which he was
acquainted with the Bible ; but it was Jerome's
Vulgate, the unadulterated original, free from the
glosses and corruptions which Rome introduced into
it at later times. Wycliffe rendered it into the clear,
nervous English of his day, child-like in its simplicity,
and often beautiful with a pathetic beauty—a language
which formed its words within itself, as German does
to the present day ; a language in which because
was *for-why*, and a promise was a *for-word*, and
redemption was *again-buying*, and soul was *in-
wit*, and immortality was *undeadliness*, and to blame
was to *under-name :* where the chief priests of the
Sanhedrim were spoken of as the bishops, and Cæsar's

palace as the moot-hall, and a steward as a baily, and a legal writ as a libel. To this day, in Wycliffe's native valley, the common people would require no explanation of the Apostle's statement in his version, that on their landing at Melita, Publius received and " found " them (Acts xxviii. 7): though modern culture might find a difficulty in comprehending such passages as "we under-fongen the behest of the Spirit " (Gal. iii. 14), or " the lightning of the science of the clearness of God " (2 Cor. iv. 6). I subjoin six verses from the Gospel of St. Matthew, and six from the Revelation, as giving a good sample of Wycliffe's style of translation.

"In that tyme ihesus answeride & seide, I know-leche to the, fadir, lord of heuene & of erthe, for thou hast hidde these thingis fro wise men & prudent : and hast schewid hem to litil children, so fadir: for so it was plesinge to fore thee, alle thingis ben gouun[1] to me of my fadir, & no man knewe the sone : but the fadir, nether ony man knewe the fadir, but the sone, & to whom the sone wolde schewe. Alle ye that traueilen & ben chargid come to me ; and I schal fulfille you. Take ye my yok on you & lerne of me for I am mylde and meke in herte : and ye schulen finde rest to youre soulis, for my yok is softe & my charge liyt.[2] "—Matt. xi. 25—30.

"I ihesus sente myn aungel to witnesse to you thes thingis in chirchis, I am the root & kyn of dauith & the schynynge morre[3] sterre, & the spirit &

[1] Given. [2] Light. [3] Morrow, *i. e.* morning.

H

the spousesse [1]: scien, come thou, & he that herith: seye come thou, & he that thirstith: come, & he that wole: take he freli the watir of liif. And I witnesse to eche man: heringe the wordis of profecie of this book, if ony man schal put to thes thingis, god schal put on him the veniauncis [2] writun in this book, & if ony man do awey of wordis of the boke of this profecie, god schal take awei the part of him fro the book of liif,[3] & fro the holi citee, & fro thes thingis that ben writun in this book, he seith that berith witnessinge of thes thingis: yhe amen, 1 come soone amen, come thou lord ihesus, the grace of oure lord ihesus crist: be with you alle amen."—Rev. xxii. 16—21.

I have here given the spelling of Wycliffe's day, as any reader can avail himself of the aid of our present version; but in quoting from the Reformer's sermons, the spelling and the obsolete words will be modernized.

It seems scarcely credible that the translation of the Bible should have taken only two years to make. There is, however, strong probability that Wycliffe was aided by various friends in this work—more especially by Hereford, Ashton, Repingdon, and Purvey, the first of whom had already translated the books of Job to Canticles inclusive, before Wycliffe began his work. This Nicholas de Hereford, an Oxford priest, was a warm friend and follower of Wycliffe; and he probably did a great deal of good, judging from the exceedingly uncomely adjectives

---

[1] *Spouse* was then a masculine word only.
[2] Vengeances.   [3] Life.

which the monkish chroniclers think appropriate to
describe him. And—a significant fact, which can be
stated but of few—he never fell away.

Modern Ritualists are given to sneering assertions
that Wycliffe was something very different from a
model Protestant of the present day. Perhaps so ;
but he was yet more different from a model Ritualist
of the present day, from whom he dissented upon far
more vital points than from the Protestant. And
Wycliffe was coming up from the darkness into the
light, as quickly as he had the power to do it, while
the scoffers are descending from the light into the
darkness. They may have reached about the same
part of the mountain, but how different are the
position and the goal!

In one of his English sermons, Wycliffe writes,—
" A great Bishop of England, as men say,[1] is evil
paid [2] that God's law is written in English, to unlearned men ; and he pursueth a priest for he writeth
to men this English, and summoneth him and
travaileth [3] him that it is hard to him to rowte.[4]
And thus he pursueth another priest by the help of
Pharisees, for he preached Christ's Gospel freely
without fables. O men that be on Christ's side, help
ye now against Antichrist! for the perilous time is
come that Christ and Paul told before. But one

---

[1] Query, see : *seien* may mean either.
[2] Discontented.   [3] Worries or teases him.
[4] A word with many meanings,—to stir up, roar out, snore,
etc. Probably Wycliffe meant what a modern writer might
express by saying, "he would not give him time to wink, or
sneeze."

H 2

comfort is of knights,[1] that they savour much the
Gospel, and have will to read in English the Gospel
of Christ's life."

Wycliffe himself is no doubt the priest first named;
the last may be Hereford, or some other of his
preaching friends.

By the spring of 1381 at the latest, Wycliffe had
arrived at that point which was the pivot of his
career. To quote the acetic words of Ralph Higden,
"This year that old hypocrite, John Wyklyf the
heretic, reasserted the detestable opinions of Berenger
concerning the sacrament of the altar, and seduced
many." A few words of explanation are desirable.

Until the seventh General Council, held at Nice in
787, it had never occurred to any Christian to doubt
that when Christ said of a piece of bread, "This is
My body," He meant nothing but "This represents
My body"—said just in the same way as a man might
now point to a portrait on the wall, and say, "That is
my father." At this council the idea was suggested
that He meant something more. But it was not
taken up, and it died away again until 831, when it
was revived by an obscure monk of Corbie, named
Paschaise Radbert. This time it met with more
notice, but the shape which the notice first took was
that of ridicule. Berenger of Tours, a pungent and
eloquent writer, treated Brother Paschaise to some
very peppery satire ; while Raban the Great, Archbishop of Mentz, denounced it as "an error and a

1. By this word he often means, in modern parlance, the
gentry.

novelty." Notwithstanding this, the idea of transubstantiation gradually took root and spread abroad, until at the fourth Lateran Council in 1215, it was formally adopted as matter of faith. Upon this point John Wycliffe was now reviving the opinions of Berenger of Tours.

It was in his old academical home, the University of Oxford, that Wycliffe first assailed the doctrine of transubstantiation. With this man, as with Luther, to recognize a doctrine as scriptural was to begin at once to preach it ; and he published his conclusions on this subject, in his favourite form of theses. They ran thus :—

I. "The consecrated host which we see on the altar is neither Christ nor any part of Him, but the efficacious sign of Him.

II. " No pilgrim upon earth is able to see Christ in the consecrated host with the bodily eye, but by faith.

III. " Formerly the faith of the Roman Church was expressed in the confession of Berenger—viz. that the bread and wine, which continue after the benediction, are the consecrated host.

IV. "The Lord's Supper, in virtue of the sacramental words, contains both the body and the blood of Christ, truly and really, at every point.

V. "Transubstantiation, Identification, and Impanation—terms made use of by those who have given names to the signs employed in the Lord's Supper—cannot be shown to have any foundation in the Word of God.

VI. " It is contrary to the opinions of the saints

to assert that in the true host there is an accident without a subject.[1]

VII. "The sacrament of the eucharist is in its own nature bread and wine, having, by virtue of the sacramental words, the true body and blood of Christ at every point of it.

VIII. "The sacrament of the eucharist is in a figure the body and blood of Christ, into which the bread and wine are transubstantiated, of which latter the nature remains the same after consecration, although in the contemplation of believers it is thrown into the background.

IX. "That an accident can exist without a subject is what cannot be proved to be well grounded ; but if this be so, God is annihilated, and every article of the Christian faith perishes.

X. "Every person or sect is heretical in the extreme which obstinately maintains that the sacrament of the altar is bread of a kind *per se*—of an infinitely lower and more imperfect kind even than horses' bread.

XI. "Whoever shall obstinately maintain that the said sacrament is an accident, a quality, a quantity, or an aggregate of these things, falls into the beforementioned heresy.

XII. "Wheaten bread, in which alone it is lawful to

---

[1] These are logical terms. The "subject" is the thing spoken of ; the "accident" signifies a condition or quality of a non-essential character. When we make an assertion concerning anything, there must be something of which to make it : *e.g. the horse* (subject) *is black* (accident). Blackness can only exist as a quality of something which is black.

consecrate, is in its nature infinitely more perfect than bread of bean flour or of bran, and both of these are in their nature more perfect than an accident."

The attention of the reader is requested to a few words in the third of these propositions, which may be passed unnoticed, and yet which are of the highest importance, as containing the very kernel of the question at issue. "The bread and wine which continue after the benediction." The very essence of transubstantiation lies in the theory, for which Rome contends to the death, that after consecration the substance of bread, and the substance of wine, are gone from the elements, and do not remain. What a man sees may look to be bread and wine, but is not so any longer; it has been essentially changed into the body and blood of Christ. This was the question on which all the Marian martyrs suffered, a hundred and thirty years afterwards. The test-question was put to each one whether he believed that after consecration, the substance of bread and wine remained on the altar; and they all replied in the affirmative. Here we find Wycliffe distinctly affirming the same thing, which he perpetually reiterates as a matter of the greatest importance.

The uproar caused by the publication of these propositions at Oxford was immense. The clerical party in the University expressed its horror and amazement in strong terms. The orthodox faith of the Church had been assailed, they cried; devout feeling among the people was impaired; the honour of the University was at stake if such doctrines were

allowed to be preached in it. The Chancellor, William
de Berton, was a member of this party. He called
together a council of twenty learned men, of whom
two were lawyers, ten doctors of divinity, and eight
friars (six being mendicants), to advise him what to
do to free the University from the scandal threatening
it. Their unanimous decision was that a decree should
be issued announcing the theses to be heretical, and
prohibiting them from being taught. The Chancellor
followed this advice, but without any personal mention
of Wycliffe in his mandate. The penalties attached
were suspension from every kind of teaching, the
greater excommunication, and imprisonment.

When the officer charged with the publication of
this mandate entered the Augustinian Monastery at
Oxford, which stood between Trinity College and
the present site of Wadham, in one of its splendid
lecture-rooms he encountered the arch-heretic himself, taken red-handed in the act, seated in the professor's chair, and lecturing on the forbidden subject.
Wycliffe was evidently startled by the mandate, but
he sturdily insisted on finishing his lecture in spite
of it.[1] Nor did he close it without a few pithy words,
which showed them the manner of man with whom
they had to deal.

"Neither shall Chancellor nor any other have
power to change my belief!"

And he appealed, not to pope or bishop, but to
king and parliament.

---

[1] Extracts from Register of Bishop Bokenham, Lansdowne
MS. 959, fol. 24.

The enemy which had silenced Wycliffe's tongue was powerless to stop his pen. From the rectory at Lutterworth came forth a Latin confession of faith, and the most famous of all his English sermons, the "Wicket." But a heavier blow was about to fall upon the Lollards than any which the prelates could have dealt. It almost seems as if Satan saw that his delegates could not manage the work, and took the matter into his own hands.

CHAPTER VI.

THE PEASANTS' WAR.—THIRD AND FOURTH TRIALS.—THE CRUSADE. 1381—1383.

ALF of the year 1381 had scarcely run out, when one of the most terrible events of the fourteenth century broke upon England without a note of warning. This was the peasants' war, the names of whose leaders, Jack Straw and Wat Tyler, are even yet as household words. Their objects, as stated by Jack Straw himself, were the death of the King—who was only fourteen years of age—and the extermination of all land-holders, prelates, endowed monks, canons, and parish priests. They meant to leave no clergy except the mendicant friars, whom they seemed to have looked upon as brethren of their own class. Nicholas de Hereford was not afraid to say boldly that the mendicant friars were at the bottom of the whole affair : in answer to which these gentry did their utmost to show that John Wycliffe and his followers were the source and abettors of the mischief. It was decidedly a bold accusation, considering that Wycliffe was himself one of the parish priests doomed to extermination, and that all his principal friends and sup-

porters would likewise have been put to death. The
insurgents professed, above all, a special hatred to
Wycliffe's great patron the Duke of Lancaster. They
took an oath from every one who joined them to
recognize no king named John, which could only
refer to him. Their very first action on marching
to London was to storm and burn the Savoy Palace,
his official residence, to shoot him in effigy, and to
destroy, not plunder, as much of his property as they
could lay their hands on. Two pieces of plate they
threw into the Thames. They staved the casks and
set eighteen tuns of wine flowing ; they flung 427 lbs.
of wax which they found in the palace into the fire
to assist its speedy destruction, and added twenty-
three loads of hay to help the blaze.[1] The Duke,
happily, was in Scotland, and stayed there till all
was over ; but the Duchess, who was at Leicester,
fled in terror, never stopping till she reached Knares-
borough, for her servants at Pomfret were too
frightened to open the gates. The Duke's physician,
though he was a Grey Friar, they murdered. John
of Gaunt's own feeling with respect to that terrible
time is shown in his Register ; he speaks of it as " the
great tumult," " the horrible tumult of the rebellious
commons." Two days later the rebels surrounded
the Tower, out of which the young King was hastily
conveyed, seized upon several officers of state and
beheaded them, the Archbishop being one, terrified
the Princess of Wales into fainting, and generally
frightened all respectable people into a panic. They

[1] Register of John of Gaunt, ii., ff. 58 b, 63 b.

also destroyed the Temple, and burnt several endowed
abbeys.   Had they particularly wished to injure the
Lollard cause, they could hardly have succeeded
better than by the cruel murder of the mild Archbishop Sudbury, a man who would have sacrificed
anything for peace, who had been dragged into the
persecution against his will, and who was even suspected in some quarters of a secret leaning to the
doctrines of Wycliffe.   His death made way for
Courtenay, the chief enemy of the Lollard party, to
reach the primacy of England.

About this time a certain priest, John Ball by
name, who was one of the insurgents, made himself
notorious by preaching most seditious doctrines, while
he complacently announced himself as a pupil of
Wycliffe, whose lectures he had been attending for
two years.   Considering that this gentleman was an
older man than the Reformer, and that he had been
preaching these delectable doctrines for twenty years,
dating back to a period before the world had heard
of Wycliffe, the assumption was somewhat incredible.
His grand theme (which was also the motto of the
insurgents, flaunted on a banner) has been preserved
in its original form.

> " When Adam delved and Eva span,
>   Who was then the gentleman ? "

It probably did not occur to these levelling intellects that Adam might have been a gentleman, notwithstanding the hypothetical spade-work attributed
to him.   Whether Ball were in reality an enemy of

Wycliffe who desired to injure him by embroiling
him in the peasants' war, or whether he were a
genuine fanatic who believed in his own delusions,
is a question the answer to which will perhaps never
be known now. Whatever were the truth, the shafts
which the enemy had so carefully elaborated only
embarrassed and tormented the witness for God.
They proved in the end powerless to destroy either
himself or the doctrine which he preached. Ball paid
the penalty of his sedition, being hanged at St. Albans
in July ; but Wycliffe kept on his way unscathed.

One result the peasants' war had as respected the
Reformer : to increase the breach which had already
been made between himself and the Mendicant Orders.
From this time his attacks upon them are neither
few nor weak. Many times he alludes to a conspiracy by them against the life of the Duke of
Lancaster, of which no mention is found in contem-
porary history, and which appears considerably to
have increased his opposition. It was probably
about the close of this year, 1381, that he issued a
tract entitled *De Nova Prevaricantia Mandatorum*,
in which he strongly urges that the Gospel, and especially the Ten Commandments, should be taught to
the people in English. Some of the diction of this
work is original and curious. The endowed clergy
he dubs "satraps and Pharisees," the mendicants
"disciples of Antichrist." Here, for the first time,
he expresses something more than a doubt of purgatory, as "having no foundation in Scripture,"
but being a fable "used by Antichrist to spoil

men" by means of "indulgences and simoniacal merchandise."

On the 9th of September Courtenay was translated to Canterbury, and he was not long in setting his wits to work on the difficult question of silencing this irrepressible man at Lutterworth. He was, however, obliged to wait his opportunity. When the revolt of the peasants was finally suppressed, the terrified country had to be calmed down, the rebels punished, and political matters to be set in train again. Beyond this, the King was about to be married, young as he was, to the most exalted Princess who had ever shared the throne of England, and the English loved to speak of the fair-haired German girl as "Cæsar's daughter." Little idea had Bishop Courtenay of the "spoke in his wheel" which that quiet, soft-spoken German maiden was to be. She landed, it is said, in the midst of a violent tempest, and she brought with her a box of pins, which the English had never seen before, and three Bibles, in Latin, German, and Bohemian. Her first act was to smile graciously upon her subjects and distribute presents among them;[1] her second to request an amnesty for the rebellious commons not yet executed;[2] her third, the cleverest move of all, to shut

---

[1] Issue Roll, Michaelmas, 5 Ric. II. The chroniclers tell us that the future Queen landed on Dec. 21st; but the Issue Roll plainly shows that on the ninth of that month she was at Leeds Castle, near Maidstone, which was a part of her queenly appanage.

[2] Pardons Roll, 5—21 Ric. II., Dec. 18, 1381; *Acta Regia*, p. 193, Dec. 13th.

Bishop Arundel's mouth by meekly laying before
that courtly prelate the three irritating volumes, and
sweetly requesting his judgment on the respective
translations. Henceforth, while Anna of Bohemia
lived, the prelates might bluster against Wycliffe,
but they could go no further. She at once recognized in him a kindred spirit, and she drove the
reluctant hierarchical team in her silken reins, laid
so lightly on their necks that there was no room to
chafe, and yet so effectually that their pace was
checked.

Just at first, Courtenay failed to recognize the
nature of this fair and soft obstacle, and pressed
forward triumphantly in his career. Under his
auspices the clergy conceded a tenth to the Crown
on condition that they should receive help " in the
destruction of the Wycliffe heretics, whose wicked doctrine had infected the whole kingdom." [1] The result
of this was twofold. On the 17th of May—the new
Archbishop was not able to act sooner, since he only
received his pallium from Rome on the sixth of that
month, and until he was invested with that sacred
robe, he did not consider himself a proper archbishop
—Courtenay gathered round him an assemblage of
ten bishops, sixteen doctors of law, thirty doctors of
divinity, and four bachelors of law. The court was
packed, the Archbishop having chosen men who were
safe to vote with him.[2] They assembled in the hall
of the monastery at Blackfriars, not (as is often

---

[1] Polychronicon Rogeri Cestrensis, Harl. MS. 1729, fol. 154.
[2] Lechler's *Wiclif*, p. 418.

asserted, from a mistranslation in the first edition of Foxe's *Acts and Monuments*, now corrected) in the church of the Austin Friars. The learned assembly having done the duty for which it was convoked, and agreed with the Archbishop, a solemn convention was appointed in the same place for the 21st of May, and the arch-heretic was cited to appear. On the day appointed, Archbishop and Council kept their tryst, but the criminal was not so obedient. The court sat, but there was no prisoner at the bar. While they were engaged in debating this astonishing fact, another agency made itself felt, to their yet greater amazement. One of the severest shocks of earthquake ever known in England rocked the hall at Blackfriars. The first feeling of the assembly was terror; but Courtenay rapidly made capital out of the occurrence, assuring the frightened doctors that it was an encouraging omen, prefiguring the purification of the Church from erroneous doctrines. Wycliffe himself made fun of the "Earthquake Council," as he termed them, but he certainly looked upon the earthquake itself as rather his friend than theirs. He speaks of it as a judgment of God on the proceedings of the assembly, or as an outcry of the earth itself against the ungodly deeds of men.

The clerical council continued its sitting, and in two days they were startled by a second earthquake. Courtenay felt it necessary to make haste, lest a superstitious panic should seize his followers. It was the more needful, because London, always a difficult item for the hierarchy to govern, was falling further

and further from him day by day. The opinion of
London ruled England at that time far more than it
now does; and several of Wycliffe's itinerant preachers
had found their way to London, and produced a
startling impression on the metropolis, which in the
eyes of the bishops was already too much imbued
with Wycliffe's views. The pulpits of the city were
taking the infection now, and since the population at
that time was only thirty-five thousand, the sensation
created was far more apparent than any similar event
would be at the present day.

But there was yet a further unpardonable offence
which Wycliffe had committed, and this touched
Courtenay more personally. Wycliffe, in conjunction
with the Lollard Lord Mayor, John de Northampton,
had presumed to stir up the Londoners to punish
certain vicious persons among them, a necessary
business which it was high time for some responsible
person to take in hand. The proceedings of the
audacious reformers of the metropolitan morals were
not by any means to be termed half measures. The
Lord Mayor seized upon some of the worst characters
in the city, of both sexes, shaved off their hair, and
led them in public disgrace through the streets, a
punishment ordinarily reserved for thieves.

Every form of moral administration was regarded
by the bishops as their peculiar province, so that this
alone was equivalent to an insult to those right
reverend individuals. But, adding insult to injury,
these utterly unqualified persons had so far forgotten
themselves as to assert that they did such things

I

because the authorized persons neglected their duty. Nor did they even stop at this enormity, for they actually went on to talk, in most unpolished terms, of the "filthy avarice" of the rightful authorities, averring that they were "choked with bribes" from the vicious individuals aforesaid, in consequence of which they were unable to perceive the scandals which were so apparent to the unblinded eyes of the Lord Mayor and the Rector of Lutterworth. This was beyond all pardon.

With a view to stop the whole work in all its ramifications, Courtenay quickly prepared and hurried through the House of Lords a Bill afterwards known as the Clerical Statute. It was entitled, "An Act to commission the Sheriffs to apprehend preachers of heresy," and it recounted that "there be divers evil persons within the realm, going from county to county, and from town to town, in certain habits, under dissimulation of great holiness, and without the licence of the ordinaries of the places or other sufficient authority, preaching daily, not only in churches and church-yards, but also in markets, fairs, and other open places, where a great congregation of people is, divers sermons containing heresies and notorious errors, . . . which persons do also preach divers matters of slander, to engender discord and dissension betwixt divers estates of the said realm, as well spiritual as temporal, to excite the people, to the great peril of all the realm ; which preachers, being cited or summoned before the ordinaries of the places, . . will not obey to their summons and commandments, nor care not for their monitions nor the censures of holy Church, but expressly despise them ; and, moreover, by their subtle and ingenious words do draw the people to hear their sermons, and do maintain them in their errors by strong hand and by great routs. It is ordained and assented in this present Parliament that the King's commissions be made and directed to the sheriffs and other ministers of our Sovereign Lord the King, or other sufficient persons learned, and according to the certifications of the prelates thereof to be made in Chancery from time to time, to arrest all such preachers, and also their fawtors, maintainers, and abettors, and to hold them in arrest and strong prison, till they will justify themselves according to reason and the law of holy Church. And the King willeth and commandeth that the Chancellor make such commissions at all times that he by the prelates or any of them shall be certified and thereto required."

This crafty proclamation, for statute it was not, requires and deserves a careful reading. The Arch-bishop did not dare to present it to the Commons, who, he well knew, would never dream of passing it ; so, having hastily smuggled it through the House of Lords, he sweetly offered it to the boy King— doubtless choosing a moment when those trouble-some persons the Princess of Wales and the Duke of Lancaster were not present—as a measure which had passed Parliament, and only required the touch of his sceptre to make it law. How was the royal youth, only just fifteen, to penetrate the dishonest shuffle of the clerical members of his Council, when at the dissolution of Parliament this Bill was presented to him among a multitude of others to receive his assent? or how were the faithful Commons at the other end of the hall to imagine that the sedate and suave prelate who sat at the head of the episcopal bench was committing a fraud upon them, just as dishonest as if he had sold them stones for bread, or had given them under weight and short measure across a shop counter?

The Clerical Statute being safely passed, Courtenay's next step was to issue, two days later (May 28th), a mandate in the King's name, commanding the arrest of the itinerant preachers, according to the petition of him, William Archbishop of Canterbury. The said unauthorized preachers were ordered to be detained in prison " until they should repent of and amend their erroneous and heretical pravities." It also pleased this Right Reverend Father to publish to the world the conclusions of the Earthquake Council, among which was a list of the articles of Wycliffe condemned by them as heretical. Some of these were the genuine theses put forth by himself; but the list also comprised the following items, which the Council must have produced either out of their inner consciousness, or by twisting Wycliffe's words to some conclusion which he never intended.

" That God ought to obey the devil.[1]

[1] " Christ is chief Lord of the fiend and all his limbs, and they must needs serve Him either well or evil, doing well that they should do, or else suffering penalty."—Arnold's *English Works*, i. 23.

"That it is against the sacred Scripture that ecclesiastical persons should have *any* temporal possessions.

"That temporal lords may *at will* take away their temporal goods from churches habitually delinquent. (This Wycliffe had distinctly denied, as we have already seen.)

"That the public may correct delinquent rulers at will."

There were other articles, very likely genuine, and less horrible in Protestant eyes than in these episcopal ones.

"That if a man be truly contrite, all exterior confession is to him superfluous and invalid.

"That it hath no foundation in the Gospel that Christ did ordain the mass.

"That any man who enters into any private religion whatever (*i. e.* any religious Order) is thereby made more unapt and unable to observe the commandments of God.

"That holy men who have instituted any private religions whatsoever (as well of seculars having possessions, as of begging friars having none), in so instituting did err.

"That religious men living in private religions are not of the Christian religion.

"That friars are bound to get their living by the labour of their hands, and not by begging."

On the 12th of June, 1382, the Archbishop issued a general inhibition, after three monitions, against Wycliffe, Hereford, Repingdon, Ashton, and Bedeman, as specially distinguished amongst other "heretics." He further issued a mandate to the Chancellor of Oxford, directing him to inhibit these five men from preaching. He was to silence all that favoured them, to publish the condemnation of Wycliffe's theses in St. Mary's Church, and either "put to their purgation, or cause to abjure"; whomsoever he took or found to be one of his adherents.

"My Lord," exclaimed the dismayed Chancellor, "I dare not to do such a thing, for fear of death!"

"What!" cried the Archbishop, "is Oxford such a nestler and favourer of heresies, that the Catholic truth cannot be published?"

The Archbishop and his Council proceeded to sit on the smaller cases. Hereford and Repingdon took flight, and, refusing to appear, were adjudged contumacious. They appealed to the Pope, but the Archbishop rejected their appeal as frivolous and insolent, and declined to forward it (the "episcopal veto" was then in full operation!); they were accordingly excommunicated. Ashton, Repingdon, and Bedeman were at last restored to communion, the two last after abjuration. Hereford stood firm, and Wycliffe declined to take the least notice of the proceedings. He was busy finishing the translation of the Bible, and writing his third polemical tract, *The Dissensions of the Popes.* Of this work both Latin and English versions were published, but the latter is very much fuller and longer. Wycliffe considered the Great Schism of the West a sign that the end of the world was approaching.

"And first it seemeth that dissension of this

popedom is for covetousness of honour and winning
of this world, that by subtlety of the fiend is knitted
to this office. For if the Pope hold cleanly that
that Christ gave to Peter, he should have goods
[in the form] of virtues, and travail with poverty,
and none of this worldly glory, since that Christ
forbade it. But who would then strive thus for
the Pope's office?"

A little further on he says, "And trust we in the
help of Christ in this point; for He hath begun to
help us graciously, in that that He hath cloven
the head of Antichrist, and made the one part
fight against the other." He urges his readers not
to mind being called heretics. "Christ Himself was
called a blasphemer, that is heretic most of all other."
Concerning the imaginary celestial treasury of saintly
merit, on which the Pope should draw at pleasure,
he utters withering words. "For then each Pope
should be lord of this heavenly treasure, and so he
should be lord of Christ and other saints in heaven,—
yea, if he were a fiend, as was Judas Iscariot. Lord!
why should God of Heaven make this fiend such a
lord?" He ends with a diatribe against the friars,
"who spoil not only the realm's treasure and men's
bodies, but they send souls to hell, and goeth
themself after."

In this tract we have the first sound of one of
the strongest blasts delivered from the trumpet of
John Wycliffe, namely, against the crusade on
behalf of Urban, which the Mendicant Orders had
warmly espoused, and for which they were beating

up recruits. The head of this crusade was Bishop Henry Le Despenser of Norwich, and it was about October, 1382, that Urban's Bull addressed to him concerning it was issued. From first to last Wycliffe condemned it in the strongest language, as a slaughter of innocent Christians, not in the cause of Christ, but as a sacrifice to the worldly ambition of the two Papal rivals.

No sooner had Parliament met again on the 6th of October, than the House of Commons asserted its outraged dignity by praying for a repeal of the so-called Clerical Statute, which had been passed without its assent and in its despite. The King in council at once commanded that the statute should be repealed accordingly.

The smaller Lollards, as the disciples of Wycliffe were beginning to be called, had now been disposed of to Courtenay's satisfaction. Of all those cited before the prelates, two only had stood firm, Wycliffe and Hereford, and the latter of these had gone into voluntary banishment. The chronicler Knighton —who was so prejudiced against the Lollards, and so much under the influence of Henry IV., that his value as an authority where they are concerned is simply *nil*, unless confirmed by more trustworthy evidence—asserts that Hereford recanted in 1382 ; but there is no confirmation of the statement, and it is sufficiently disproved by his disappearance. Had he recanted, why should he have fled ? The same chronicler tells us that Hereford went to Rome, and laid the matter before Pope Urban himself, who confirmed the judgment of the English prelates, and graciously sentenced Hereford, not to death at the stake, but to imprisonment for life. He adds that in the summer of 1385, in consequence of a riot in which the Papal prison was thrown open, Hereford escaped and returned home. What is certain is that Hereford never finished his translation of the Old Testament, abruptly broken off at his trial ; that in 1383 Archbishop Courtenay appealed to the King against him, because " he was still setting the ban pronounced upon him at defiance ;" that in 1387 he was the leader of the Lollard itinerant preachers in England, and that in 1391 he was in Court favour, shown by a grant of trees for fuel. So far as we know, not one hair fell from the head of this bold and faithful Protestant.

But one man remained to be dealt with, and this was the " arch-heretic" himself. For the fourth time the Archbishop cited Wycliffe before his tribunal, this time held in the cathedral church of St. Frideswide, Oxford, on the 18th of November, 1382. It is uncertain whether the Reformer obeyed the citation or not ; the balance of evidence appears to be on the affirmative side. But it is certain that he addressed a petition to King and Parliament, wherein he dealt with four points and his opinions thereon. The four points may be thus stated :—

1. That all religious Orders are of man's invention, and therefore the vows are not binding on any who desire to withdraw.

2. That those men that unreasonably and wrong-

fully have damned [*i. e.* condemned] all this Council, be amended of so great error, and that their error may be published to men dwelling in the realm.

3. That tithes, having been originally paid according to God's law, should now be withdrawn by the same.

4. That Christ's and the Apostles' teaching concerning the Sacrament may be taught openly in churches, to Christian people.

The date of this petition is one of the most difficult points to settle in Wycliffe's life. Some writers place it in May, during the session of the first Parliament of 1382; some after July, when Wycliffe's friends had been condemned at Oxford; some in November, during the second session. All that can be said on this head is that the later date seems more likely than the earlier. There may possibly have been two petitions; but in this case, unless they were identically worded, only one is extant.

Most of Wycliffe's biographers assert that John of Gaunt himself went down on purpose from London to Oxford, to entreat, or rather to command, that Wycliffe would withdraw the appeal, and submit to the judgment of Convocation. I cannot help thinking this story excessively improbable,—not in respect of the advice, but of the journey. As Parliament was also sitting at Oxford, it is almost certain that the Duke of Lancaster was there already: in which case a costly and arduous journey did not need to be taken. For the advice he is warmly commended in Archbishop Sudbury's Register: and as he is

known not to have shared Wycliffe's eucharistic
opinions, it is by no means improbable that he gave
it, in the interests alike of peace and of Wycliffe himself. But though the counsel may have been given,
it was not taken. The judges sat as intended—
Canterbury, with six of his suffragans—the Bishops
of Lincoln, Norwich, Worcester, London, Salisbury,
and Hereford. Three at least of them, beside the
Archbishop, were no friends of Wycliffe. Braybroke
of London was among the persecutors; Gilbert of
Hereford belonged to the orthodox party; and Le
Despenser of Norwich was not likely to desire the
special welfare of the man who was so bitterly opposing that crusade of which he was the chief leader.

Wycliffe delivered to Convocation, probably in
person, a Latin confession, wherein he once more
definitely stated his views upon the eucharist. There
were six senses, he said, in which it was possible
for the body of Christ to be anywhere present:
virtually, spiritually, sacramentally, corporeally, sub-
stantially, and dimensionally. After the first three
manners, Christ was present in the Sacrament; after
the last three, He could be present, during this
dispensation, only in Heaven.

The usual "conclusion in which nothing was
concluded" followed this last trial of John Wycliffe.
Convocation abstained from pronouncing any judgment. Knighton asserts that it was because the
prisoner at the bar recanted his errors; but unfortunately for himself, he gives the confession entire, which
proves not to contain a line of retractation, but

simply a full and clear statement of the contrary
views held by the Reformer !

For a little while it seemed as though this would
be the last action of John Wycliffe. Before he could
return home, and while in London, he was laid low
by a paralytic stroke. His enemies were delighted
with what they deemed a providential interference on
their behalf; and various mendicant friars gathered
around what was thought to be the bed of death,
perhaps in the hope of hearing some recantation of
his opinions. "And when they had babbled much
unto him," Wycliffe suddenly sat up in his bed, and
gave them his answer.

"I shall not die, but live, and declare the works of
the Lord !"[1]

The disease appears to have left him completely
for the time. He recovered, to preach more strongly
than before, to pour forth volumes with greater
rapidity than ever. During the year now opening,
so far as can be gathered from internal evidence,
he published at least six of his Latin polemical
works. They were entitled, *The Orders of Friars,
The Three Chains of Love, The Standard of Perfection, The Crusade, The Four New Orders,* and *The
Foundation of the Orders.*

The Crusade is one of Wycliffe's longest works.
He thunders against Pope and Antipope, temporal
power and spiritual tyranny, the Crusade and the

---

[1] A later and more sensational version of the story makes
him say, instead of " the works of the Lord," "the evil deeds of
the friars."

friars who preached in its favour. With pungent
sarcasm he impales the advocates of the Crusade on
one of the two horns of the dilemma, that either Christ
or the Papacy must have made a blunder, and have
acted imprudently. They can take which conclusion
they please, but in his opinion, to one of the two
they must come.

But among the most interesting of Wycliffe's works
is *The Three Chains of Love*, since it treats of other
and a greater variety of subjects than most of his
polemical tracts. The "three chains" are natural,
conjugal, and spiritual love : the first has its source
in the love of God the Father to His creatures, the
second in that of God the Son to His Church, and
the third in that of the Holy Ghost, who is the bond
of charity uniting Christians to one another. In the
course of his argument he brings in side-issues of
an interesting kind : *e.g.* he has heard that "the
noble Queen of England, the sister of Cæsar, possesses the Gospels in three languages, Bohemian,
German, and Latin, and would not he who should
insinuate therefore that she is a heretic be guilty of
the pride of Lucifer? And if," dexterously adds
the Evangelical Doctor, "the Germans may reasonably have Scripture in their own language, it is
reasonable that the English ought to have it likewise." But it is not long before he is at his usual
work, fervent denunciation of the mendicant friars,
who annually plunder the kingdom of forty thousand
pounds, which they expend in sumptuous edifices
and personal superfluities, while they are strong,

healthy men, who ought to work for their bread like others. Among other "usurpations" of these hypocrites he ranks letters of fraternity, whereby they sold their prayers for money, and the superstitious notion which they sedulously cultivated in the popular mind, that any person dying in the habit of their Order was safe for Heaven.

In *The Foundation of the Orders* his wrath waxes hot. The mendicants are "false brethren, pseudo-brethren, hypocrites, antichrists, devils." In *The Four New Orders* he complains that the prelates and endowed priests possess what ought to belong to the State; the monks do not fulfil their vows, and have made their vow of poverty a curse to the genuine poor; the canons tell falsehoods concerning their supposed foundation by St. Augustine, their miracles, and their saints; the mendicants alienate the people from the true faith, by opposing the preaching of the Gospel, and by refusing taxes to the Crown. The bishops are superfluous, says the Reformer boldly: presbyters could fulfil all their duties, and did so in the primitive Church for three hundred years: instead of preaching the Word of God, they place it lower than the Rule of Sarum. The Hospitallers, the chantries, the canons, the friars —all should be abolished. Even the Universities have done more harm than good. The King ought to be the universal patron, and if any priest prove unworthy, let him be removed and replaced by the State. Christ teaches that tribute should be paid to Cæsar, but He nowhere commands it to be given to Peter or to the

Pope. If the four Orders will return to the Order of Christ, let them continue to exist : some as parish priests, some as teachers and evangelists, some as artisans. And if, concludes the Reformer, it can be shown that I have erred, either by Scripture or reason, I am ready to revoke my error with all humility.

Again, in *The Standard of Perfection*, he rebukes the friars for kidnapping youths, for holding their own traditions higher than Scripture, and for preferring obedience to their monastic superiors rather than obedience to God.

The Crusade against which Wycliffe had fought so boldly set forth from Sandwich in May, 1383, the Mendicant Orders and the hierarchy having made enormous efforts to set it on foot and to beat up recruits for it. The bishops alone subscribed a ton of gold towards its expenses. In June news came of success ; but it proved only temporary, for in August, and again in October, followed utter defeat.

There were two Parliaments in 1383, in the first of which the Crusade had been resolved on, after a warm debate upon the subject. But in the latter, at the close of the year, the Commons went so far as to impeach the Bishop of Norwich, the leader of the Papal forces ; and on the 9th of January, 1384, we find the Duke of Lancaster at the head of an army in Thanet, waiting to pass to Flanders, to oppose the crusading force.[1]

[1] Issue Roll, Michaelmas, 9 Ric. II.—We have it on Wycliffe's

It has been usual to represent the Duke as a great
friend to the Mendicant Orders.   It is, however, somewhat questionable how far this is true.   What affection he may have had for mendicants was not likely
to be increased by the conspiracy of Latimer, a
Carmelite friar, who took upon him to accuse the
Duke of high treason in the summer of 1383.   The
result was nothing except to himself; to him it was
death at the hands of the Duke's son-in-law, Sir John
de Holand, who took upon himself to administer
lynch law after a barbarous manner, neither the King
nor the Duke knowing anything about it until all
was over.

The crusading army did not retire from the field
" in excellent order"—in any sense of the words.
Judging from the conduct of some among them, the
character of the warriors was not unexceptionable.
An entry on the Close Roll, under date of March
6th, 1384, records the underhand proceedings of Sir
William de Elmham during this expedition, he having
received " from our enemies of France, under colour
of treating for peace, without our licence," the enormous sum of three thousand four hundred francs.[1]

The Government was of Wycliffe's opinion in
respect to one question.   On the 2nd of November,
1383, a proclamation had been issued which must
have given him satisfaction, whereby the King's pleasure was declared against the admission of aliens to

own authority that the King and John of Gaunt were personally
no favourers of the Crusade.   (Arnold's *English Works*, III.
386.)   [1] Close Roll, 7 Ric. II.

any English benefice, on account of the " damage and inconvenience thereby accruing to our royal crown and to the Anglican Church." The arch-bishops, bishops, abbots, priors, deans, archdeacons, and all other persons, were charged "neither to attempt nor to suffer to be attempted any similar damage, under any art or colour whatever, against the Crown, the Anglican Church, and the laws, customs, and statutes of our realm of England." [1]

Some comfort was needed by the Rector of Lutter-worth, whose health, already undermined by the stroke of paralysis which he had suffered in London, began to weaken and threatened to break up altogether. He found it necessary to take a curate, John Horn by name, who proved a helpful and affectionate Joshua to this aged Moses. By the tone of his con-temporaries' remarks we perceive that the Reformer was now an old man ; not improbably an unusually old man for that day. He had also near him another friend and helper, in the person of John Purvey, who is believed to have been of material assistance to him in the translation of the Bible, and in the revision of it after Wycliffe's death. It is probably to Horn and Purvey that we owe the preservation of so many of Wycliffe's sermons.

The tale of one portion of the Reformer's life is now complete; so far as he is concerned the story of the persecution is over. Whether some personal influence were brought to bear on the individual members of the hierarchy, and especially on the

---

[1] Close Roll, 7 Ric. II.

K

Archbishop ; whether they were afraid of Council or of Parliament, or whether they felt that their enemy's time could not now be long, Courtenay held his hand, and what he initiated the rest were sure to follow. A breathing-time, which he made a working-time, was permitted to John Wycliffe before he was summoned to his eternal rest. The Lord stayed His rough wind in the day of the east wind.

CHAPTER VII.

"WHERE BEYOND THESE VOICES THERE IS PEACE."

HE clergy were now allowed a breathing-space ; but the Protestant laity were not so happy. The year 1384 had but just opened, when fresh anxieties came to Wycliffe, not on his own account, but on that of his colleague and friend, John de Northampton.

If a score of well-read men were asked to name the famous Lord Mayors of London during the fourteenth century, it is probable that two names would be given with little hesitation—those of William Walworth and Richard Whittington. But how many of the voices would mention John de Northampton, who in all that constitutes true greatness was a greater man than either ?

Comparatively little of his history can be dis-covered, and scarcely anything has hitherto been known. Diligent research, chiefly among contem-porary MSS., has brought to light the following facts and inferences.

From what part of the country he originally came is uncertain, but it was apparently either North-amptonshire or Cambridgeshire. Nor is it quite proved whether the name by which he is known, " De Northampton," was that of his family, or a personal soubriquet affixed to himself by the citizens of London. The fact that all his relatives except his own son bore a different name may point to the latter inference, though it may indicate that he was related by the mother's side only to Robert and William de Comberton, his brothers.[1] The Lord Mayor was to all appearance a young man—perhaps about five-and-thirty, or even less—when he attained the highest civic office. He married, in or before 1375, a lady named Petronilla,[2] from whom he derived much of his landed property in the metropolis.[3] His trade was that of a draper;[4] he served as sheriff in 1376[5] and 1384,[6] and in 1381 and 1382 he was Lord Mayor.[7] It was in the latter year, as we saw in the last chapter, that, having been strongly impressed by the preaching of Wycliffe's itinerant priests, he joined the Reformer in an attempt to purify the morals of the City, and thereby drew upon both the anger of the bishops. Courtenay, who had now let Wycliffe slip through his fingers, found compensation in hunting John de Northampton to the death. There were several members of the King's Council through

[1] Close Roll, 7 Ric. II., compared with Inq. Post Mort., 10 Hen. IV., 44. He is called by Stow John de Combarton *or* Northampton.

[2] Inq. Post Mort., 8 Ric. II., 77, m. 5.

[3] *Ibid.*, m. 2 ; Close Roll, 8 Ric. II.

[4] Close Roll, 8 Ric. II., Patent Roll, *ib.*, Part 1.

[5] Stow's *Survey of London*, p. 190.

[6] Close Roll, 8 Ric. II.   [7] Stow's *Survey*, p. 190.

whom he could easily work, but not yet through Gloucester,[1] who was soon to become his most powerful and valuable tool. That Prince was still ostensibly a friend of the reforming party. Wycliffe did not live to see him otherwise, and how far he was from exhibiting his real character at this time is shown by the fact that the Reformer dedicated one of his books to him.[2] It was only too easy, also, to blind the youthful King, now about seventeen, whose saddest weakness all through his thorny life was that he found it impossible to suspect the good faith of any man who could put on a mask. On the 9th of February, 1384, an order was issued in the King's name for 'the arrest of the sheriff, John de Northampton. The mandate is addressed to Sir Nicholas Brembre, then Lord Mayor, the deadly enemy of Northampton, and it states that in consequence of information given to the Crown " of riot and insurrection of people in the City against our peace, to the great peril of us and of our kingdom," which riot can be traced to " the excitation of John de Northampton," the King commands him to arrest the said John and send him to Corfe Castle, " until we, with the advice of our Council, shall order his deliverance." [3] At that place, in the following June, he was joined by two other prisoners, his brother Robert de Comberton, and John de Blyton.[4] Without

[1] Prince Thomas of Woodstock was now Earl of Buckingham, and was not created Duke of Gloucester until Aug. 6th, 1385. The latter, however, is the name by which he is best known.

[2] Vaughan's *Life of Wycliffe*, p. 157.

[3] Close Roll, 7 Ric. II.   [4] *Ibid.*

entering here into many minor details, interesting
rather to the biographer of Northampton than of
Wycliffe, it may be shortly stated that on the 3rd
of August the former was ordered to Reading, to
appear before the Council on the 17th of that month.[1]
In the mean time, however, something had happened
at Corfe, in which the Mayor and several of the
Castle garrison were engaged,[2] which looks very like
an attempt to rescue the prisoners. A counter-order
was hastily sent to Philip Walweyn, Governor of
Corfe Castle, bidding him to keep his prisoners in
"safe security";[3] and on the 20th of August all
the goods of John de Northampton were declared
forfeited,[4] the prisoner being remanded to a second
sitting of the Council at Westminster on the 9th of
September.[5]   On that day he was once more remanded to the 12th;[6] and then he was arraigned
for the last time, in the Tower, not now before
the Council, but before a bench of eight persons,
appointed judges for the occasion.[7]   At their
head sat one of the most prominent Lollards in
the realm, Sir John de Montacute, Seneschal of
the Household; but as any three of them were to
constitute a quorum, his solitary vote was not of
much value; the rest were of the legal profession,
and among them was Robert Tresilian, whom his
enemies accuse of cruelties rivalling those of Judge

[1] Close Roll, 8 Ric. II.   [2] *Ibid.*
          [3] *Ibid.*   [4] *Ibid.*   [5] *Ibid.*
[6] Inq. Post Mort., 8 Ric. II., 77 ; Close Roll, 9 Ric. II.   .
                [7] Patent Roll, 8 Ric. II., Part 1.

Jeffries. With this prisoner were arraigned two others, Richard Norbury and John Atte More, citizens and mercers of London, who had been arrested on the 20th of August, and, as it would appear, in consequence of the disturbance at Corfe Castle. Were they too "heretics" whom, like John de Northampton, the chief priests had delivered for envy? or if they were real criminals, did the Lollard prisoner think of another captive, who was led between two malefactors to be put to death? For he was not above his Master, and the sentence passed upon all the accused was death.[1] The charge on which the sheriff was arraigned was a strange one. He was accused of conspiracy against the life of Sir Nicholas Brembre, then Lord Mayor, and with "going about the city, with crowds of people following him, in a seditious manner." Brembre— as the indictment further stated—prepared to stop this practice, when one John Costantyn, "calling upon the mob to stand by him, raised a great commotion."[2] Brembre seized and beheaded Costantyn,[3] despite of the mob, which, it would therefore appear, did not stand by him in any formidable manner. When he heard this charge first, at Reading, Northampton stood up and defended himself with spirit; asking what right the Council had to try him in the

---

[1] Close Roll, 8 Ric. II. [2] Carte, ii. 571.
[3] The head of John Costantyn, beheaded by Nicholas Brembre, late Mayor, and by him set on Ludgate, was delivered with his body to Alice his widow for burial, Feb. 25th, 1388 (Close Roll, 11 Ric. II.).

absence of its chief member, the Duke of Lancaster, who was at that time on the border, treating of peace with Scotland. The enemies of the Duke were delighted to seize this handle, and to represent him to the confused and perplexed young King as a person not to be trusted, being so manifestly in league with sowers of sedition. The matter was made worse by my Lord Thomas of Woodstock rushing into the King's presence, with a violent adjuration that he would fight any living creature, his royal nephew not excepted, who should presume to utter a doubt of his brother's impeccability ; but it was at last brought to a settlement in the wiser hands of the Princess of Wales, who, though she had grown so stout that she could scarcely mount her horse, contrived to ride to and fro, between the perplexed King and the angry Duke, until she had " brought them at one."

When arraigned at the Tower, Northampton stood mute, and did not attempt to defend himself. He saw it was of no use. He and Norbury remained at the Tower until the next day, when an order was issued to Sir Thomas Morieux, the Constable, to deliver them to the custody of John Elmingham, " that he may take them whither we and our Council have commanded." [1]

On the 7th of November, John Blyton was released from prison, the Abbot of Colchester being his bail in a hundred pounds—equal in value to about £1800 now ; and on the 8th of December, Robert de Comberton was permitted similar liberty, William Earl of

[1] Close Roll, 8 Ric. II.

Salisbury having become bail for him in the like sum.[1] To Richard de Norbury, kept prisoner in Corfe Castle, was granted, on the 31st of March, 1385, " of the King's special grace, in reverence of God and of the passion of Jesus Christ, this Good Friday, of our alms," twenty-six marks by the year for his "victualling," and ten for his clothing and other necessary expenses, to be recovered from outstanding debts owed to him on the day of his conviction.[2] The sentence of death was commuted in all three cases. The John More, mercer, of London, who was tried with Northampton, is probably identical with the John More, mercer, ordered to appear before Council at Easter, 1398.[3]

John de Northampton, Walsingham states, was condemned to " perpetual prison a hundred miles from London," which sentence was carried out at Tintagel Castle, Cornwall. According to the better evidence of the Patent Roll, the distance was eighty leagues.[4] On the 20th of December following his conviction, a grant of fifty marks per annum was made to his wife Petronilla, from the property belonging to herself at the Stillyard, in the city of London, for her own sustenance and that of her little children, with no payment of rent to the Crown.[5]

[1] Close Roll, 8 Ric. II.
[2] Patent Roll, 8 Ric. II., Part 2.—Twenty-six marks are £17 6s. 8d., equal, according to the present value of money, to about £300 in our own day.
[3] Close Roll, 21 Ric. II., Part 2.
[4] Patent Roll, 14 Ric. II., Part 1.
[5] Patent Roll, 8 Ric. II., Part 2.

One of these children was James de Northampton,
who married but died issueless in 1409, and such
of his father's lands as were then in his possession
passed to the daughters of his uncle, William de
Comberton.[1]

When King Richard came into power, one of his
early acts was to pardon Northampton and his fellow-
prisoners. On the 28th of July, 1390, the ex-Mayor
was released from prison ; and on the 2nd of
December, at the petition of the House of Commons, the sentence against him was "totally revoked
and annulled." [2]   He survived his release seven years.

No light heart could John Wycliffe have carried
through this his last year, while time after time the
news of his friends' suffering was borne to his ears,
and he knew not how soon their experience might
become his own.   But the old energy never flagged,
and the trumpet gave forth a sound as decided as it
had ever done. *The Loosing of Satan* and *Christ
and his adversary Antichrist* came forth this year,
stronger if it be possible than his previous polemical
writings.   Here he calls the Pope "our western
Antichrist" as plainly as man can do so. He com-
pares the practice of Christ with that of Antichrist—
the truth, the simplicity, the meekness, the zeal, the
submission to earthly authority, the self-sacrifice, the
liberality, the lowliness of the Master, with the falsehood and craft, the worldly magnificence, the cruelty,
the self-seeking and unsociability, the arrogant claims,

[1] Inq. Post Mort., 10 Hen. IV., 44.
[2] Patent Roll, 14 Ric. II., Part I.

the disloyalty, the avarice of him who professed to be the servant of the servants of God. The conclusion drawn is that he who desires to be a follower of Christ must be as far as he can from imitating the Pope.

Still sermon after sermon poured forth from that ever-working manufactory at Lutterworth, which the bishops would have been so delighted to destroy. They—the sermons, not the bishops!—grew more and more evangelical as the end was neared. It might almost seem as if Wycliffe knew that his time was short, and was anxious at any cost to himself to finish so far as he might the purification of the Church, which would sorely miss his wise and resolute hand.

On the 20th of September the King addressed a mandate to Archbishop Courtenay, commanding him to make a return of the value of all benefices in his diocese occupied by aliens, with the names, state, and condition of the persons so enjoying them, before the feast of St. Martin, namely, the 11th of November.[1] This would certainly be in the eyes of Wycliffe a step in the right direction.

One difficult question remains to be dealt with. Until lately it was thought a proved fact that Pope Urban VI. cited Wycliffe to appear before him at Rome in or about 1383. Some writers went so far as to say that he obeyed the citation; others pointed to a passage in the document generally called a Letter to Pope Urban, as showing that the Reformer was prevented from doing so by the first stroke of

[1] Close Roll, 8 Ric. II.

paralysis which he suffered in 1382. The best writers on Wycliffe, and notably Professor Lechler, are now of opinion that the journey was never taken, and not only this, but that the citation itself is doubtful. The so-called letter is evidently a manifesto addressed to his English friends ; and the language of the paragraph adduced simply goes to show that the Reformer would not have objected to clear himself at the Pope's tribunal, had the opportunity offered itself, and had he been able to take advantage of it. As to other legends of · a banishment or a journey to Bohemia, they are pronounced by Dr. Lechler to be mere fancies of Polydore Vérgil in the sixteenth century.[1] It is not proved that Wycliffe was ever out of England except during his mission to Bruges in 1374, and it seems certain that the last two years of his life were spent in the peace and retirement of his rectory at Lutterworth.

Shortly after the circumstances last narrated, some movement on the part of the French sent the Government into a panic. It was probably my Lord Thomas of Woodstock who was mainly responsible for it, since he hated the French intensely, and in the absence of his brother of Lancaster he always did his utmost to be master of the Council. The language, too, is very like the violent diction in which he usually indulged. The invaders—the writer was not precise in stating whom they might be—would overrun the whole kingdom, and thrust the natives out. The English

[1] Lechler's *Wiclif,* pp. 454—457.

language would be destroyed, and a new tongue
introduced ; to be followed by a general massacre
of all the inhabitants, without regard to sex, age,
or position. The Archbishop of Canterbury was
therefore earnestly desired to pray for peace.[1] If
Courtenay had prayed for the spirit of peace to
descend upon himself and Prince Thomas, it would
have tended more to the pacification of the kingdom
than a thousand diatribes against the French. He
was once more pursuing Alice Lady Windsor, left
unprotected by her husband's recent death, and particularly open to persecution, since, if we may credit
the assertion, he had died heavily in debt to the
Crown. She was compelled to "acknowledge" a
liability of six thousand pounds to Sir John de
Holand, which she was commanded to pay by
Michaelmas 1385, on the penalty of having her
goods distrained for it if payment were not forth-
coming.[2] Little is known of Alice Periers subse-
quently to this date. She retired into obscurity, not
into peace, for her lands were " annexed " by her late
husband's nephew and heir, John de Windsor, a fact
to which she alludes with some bitterness in her will :
" for, on the pain of my soul, he hath no right there,
nor never had I "[3] She died about the close of 1400,
and lies buried in Upminster Church.[4]

[1] Close Roll, 8 Ric. II.—A portion of this language is a
common formula in speaking of anticipated invasions; but in
this instance the terms used are much stronger than usual.

[2] *Ibid.*   [3] *Testamenta Vetusta*, p. 153.

[4] *Ibid.;* Addit. MS. 6076, art. Testamenta.—Dr. Vaughan,
in his life of Wycliffe, justly remarks that " Alice Perrers was

It is the custom of modern writers to charge all such exactions and oppressions on the youthful King, and to say that his extravagant expenditure necessitated their existence. Nothing can be more unjust than such a statement. The King was not extravagant compared with other monarchs, as any one may see who chooses to read his Issue Rolls; and he never had the reins of power in his own hands until 1389.

All these events must have helped to darken the cloud in which the sun was setting at Lutterworth. Two of the Rector's friends were still spared to him, his old fellow-worker, Purvey, and his faithful curate, John Horn. But all the rest were either dead or banished. It was time for John Wycliffe to rest too.

On Innocents' Day, 1384, he attended mass in Lutterworth Church as usual, and spoke to some one as he came in. Little they can have thought, who watched the steps of the old man, with the long white hair, bearing his silver-headed staff, that it was the last time they would ever watch him in this world. The Rector did not officiate; Mr. Horn performed the whole service. But just after the words of consecration were pronounced, and as the curate was

---

no doubt greatly calumniated; Walsingham appears to have recorded every malicious rumour he could learn respecting this woman " (i. 331). Seeing the intensity of Walsingham's animus, not only against the Lollards, but against all who lay under the "suspicion of being suspected" as such, it is strange that a greater number of writers have not guessed the reason of his unconcealed hatred of Alice Periers, nor thought it worth their while, and required by justice, to investigate the real facts of the case.

elevating the paten, the Rector, who sat in his customary chair at the north end of the holy table, was seen to sink heavily to the ground. Kindly hands were about the old man in an instant, seeking to know from himself what his sudden ailment might be. But it was too sadly apparent that a second stroke of paralysis had deprived the Reformer of all power of speech. The radiant eyes glanced from one to another, showing that the spirit within was as unclouded as ever ; but the powerful voice which had rocked the throne of the Vatican had uttered its last word, till it should burst into the new song of Moses and of the Lamb.

They carried him out in the communion chair, and laid him upon his own bed. Vainly, intently, lovingly, they watched for the power of speech to return. There were only three days of that tender watching, and then, on the last evening of 1384, without any farewell to those he left behind, God called John Wycliffe to the joys of Paradise.

What a rest it must have been ! No more warring against principalities and powers, and rulers of the darkness of this world ; no more vexing of that righteous soul with the ungodly deeds of the "four sects" ; no more wars and rumours of war, persecutions and endless apprehensions of persecution. What a change, to company that was sinless, a home whence he should go no more out, a moral atmosphere of perfect peace and of unsullied holiness!

The atmosphere of the world which he left behind

was of a very different character. Truly, this prophet had so tormented them that dwelt on the earth that their rejoicings over his grave were neither few nor feigned. Hear his grand enemy, the monk Thomas of Walsingham, on whose chronicle modern popular English history is built, rather than on any other, for the period comprised in it.

"On the feast of the passion of St. Thomas of Canterbury, John Wycliffe—that organ of the devil, that enemy of the Church, that author of confusion to the common people, that idol of heretics, that image of hypocrites, that restorer of schism, that storehouse of lies, that sink of flattery[1]—being struck by the horrible judgment of God, was struck with palsy, and continued to live in that condition until St. Sylvester's Day, on which he breathed out his malicious spirit into the abodes of darkness."[2] Many other choice quotations might be given, but this is about the finest flower of Papal rhetoric which blossomed over John Wycliffe's tomb.

It particularly delighted the monks to assert that it was on the day of St. Thomas of Canterbury that Wycliffe had sustained his second stroke of paralysis. The poetical justice of this coincidence might fairly be questioned, since Wycliffe, though he questioned Becket's saintliness, had always spoken with respect of him, for, as he believed and took some pains to

---

[1] It would be interesting to know who had ever been the object of Wycliffe's flattery, one of the last faults of which he could justly be accused.

[2] Quoted in Lechler's *Wiclif*, p. 460.

prove, Becket did not advocate the Pope's supremacy as against that of the King; but, unfortunately for the denouncers of judgment, the day was a mistake! That it was Innocents' Day, December 28th, and not St. Thomas's, the 29th, we have the best possible authority, that of John Horn, who in 1441, when an old man of eighty, dictated to Dr. Thomas Gascoigne an account of the last days of his revered master, and attested its truth on oath.

Thirty years after the death of John Wycliffe, the very same "judgment" fell on another man, who had been one of his chief persecutors, Thomas Arundel, at that time Archbishop of Canterbury. It need scarcely be said that the monkish chroniclers did not see it in the same light, and this time it was the Lollards who whispered that the man who died speechless had "bound the Word of the Lord." No such comment could be uttered of John Wycliffe.

They buried the Reformer in peace in his own church of Lutterworth; but his bones were not permitted a long repose, nor his memory any rest from obloquy. Arundel, when archbishop, thundered an excommunication against this " notorious heretic, who died obstinate in his heresy"; but little the blessed soul cared for that in the courts of the Lord. The Council of Constance, in 1415, indignant that "his doctrine had poisoned all Bohemia," passed sentence that his remains should be exhumed and burnt,—poor, pitiful vengeance of men who had no more that they could do!—and in 1428, in the presence of Richard Fleming, Bishop of Lincoln, the bones of

L

Wycliffe were dug up and burnt to ashes,[1] the relics being cast into the Swift, under the arch of the bridge nearest to the town. The Swift bore them to the Avon—

> "The Avon to the Severn runs,
> The Severn to the sea,
> And Wycliffe's dust shall spread abroad,
> Wide as the world shall be!"

Even then, thirty years after his voice had been stilled in death, evidence remains to show that his parishioners at Lutterworth had regarded him with a heart-veneration which, had he fought for Rome instead of Christ, would have gone far to earn him canonization. Legends sprang up and took root among them, to the effect that no water would flow under that arch where Wycliffe's ashes had been flung; and that on the spot where one of his bones had fallen sprang "St. John's Well," which still runs clear and abundant, never drying up even in the hottest seasons.

Another well was cleared by the hands of John Wycliffe, which has never hitherto run dry. At first a little spring, which for a century and a half did not exhibit itself on the surface, that pure stream of Gospel truth in the sixteenth century gushed up to light, and has since spread, a mighty life-giving lake, over the greater part of Europe. Alas that more than once the shepherds have fouled with their feet the stream at which the flock should drink, flinging back into it some of the rubbish which Wycliffe took such pains to clear away!

---

[1] Antiquitates de Lindley, Addit. MS. 6046, fol. 26, b.

In the immediate sense, Wycliffe never succeeded in inaugurating an English Reformation. But in a better and larger sense he may be styled the father of all the Reformations; for, as regards second causes, without Wycliffe there would have been no Huss, and possibly without Huss there would have been no Luther. It was the works of Wycliffe, secretly carried into Bohemia, and as secretly circulated there among all classes, which kept the sacred fire living upon the altar, until it burst forth into the flame which lighted up the world. So much can one man do! Nay, let me correct myself; so much can God do with one man!

It may be well to add a few words concerning the personal character and scholarship of Wycliffe, as showing the light in which they appeared to those of his own day. William Thorpe, one of his warmest disciples, shall be first quoted.

"Master John Wickliffe was holden of full many men the greatest clerk[1] that they knew then living; and therewith he was named a passing ruly[2] man, and an innocent in his living; . . the most virtuous and godly wise man that I heard of or knew."[3]

Let us now look at the same picture drawn by one of his bitterest enemies, Canon Knighton of Leicester.

"He came to be reckoned inferior to none of his time in philosophy, and incomparable in the performance of school exercises,[4] a man of profound wit,[5] and very strong and powerful in disputations, and by the

---

[1] The most learned man. [2] Strict, regular.
[3] Foxe, *Acts and Monuments*, Pratt's Town-end's ed., iii. 258.
[4] Scholastic philosophy. [5] Intellect.

common sort of divines esteemed little less than a god."[1]

Lastly, let us listen to the University of Oxford, the University which was Wycliffe's *Alma Mater*, which had seen him go in and out for forty years, which had silenced his voice in her stately halls, and had suffered him to be denounced as a heretic within the walls of her Cathedral. These are the words which honesty and honour wrung from her, two-and-twenty years after John Wycliffe had rested from his labours.

" With one heart, voice, and testimony we witness all his conduct throughout his whole life to have been praiseworthy ; whose honest manners, profound scholarship, and redolent fame and sweetness we earnestly desire to be known to all the faithful ; for we hold his ripe conversation and assiduous labours to tend to the praise of God, the salvation of others, and the benefit of the Church. We therefore signify unto you by these presents that his conversation, from tender years up to the time of his death, was so excellent and honest, that never was there any annoyance or sinister suspicion or infamy reported of him ; but in answering, reading, preaching, he behaved himself laudably, as a strong champion of the faith, vanquishing those who by voluntary beggary blas- phemed Christ's religion, by Catholic sentences out of Holy Scripture. Nor was the aforesaid doctor convicted of heresy, nor burned of our prelates after burial.[2] God forbid that by our prelates a man of such probity should be condemned for a heretic, who

---

[1] Quoted by Professor Burrows, *Wiclif's Place in History*, p. 4.
[2] This was written twenty-two years before the burning of Wycliffe's bones.

wrote in logic, philosophy, divinity, morality, and the speculative sciences, without his peer, as we believe, in all our University."[1]

Not the least of the remarkable facts connected with Wycliffe is to be found in the words which he uttered, almost amounting to a mysterious prescience, that a successor who should carry on his work was decreed in Heaven, and, strangest of all, that this successor should spring from one of those very Mendicant Orders against which he had struggled and thundered for some six years before his death. Dare we go so far as to say that to the dying eyes of the Rector of Lutterworth was permitted, dim and vague as it might be, a vision of the monk of Wittemberg who was to shake the world, when he wrote: "I anticipate that some of the friars whom God shall be pleased to enlighten will return with all devotion to the original religion of Christ, will lay aside their unfaithfulness, and with the consent of Antichrist, offered or solicited, will freely return to primitive truth; and then will they build up the Church, as Paul did before them"? On one point Wycliffe was misled. There was no "consent of Antichrist," nor any possibility of it! From his eyes were hidden the hecatombs of martyrs through whose blood the Church passed to her primitive purity, and who, though the document might be drawn up by Wycliffe and Huss and Luther, were the red seals which stamped it with validity and permanence.

And now that five hundred years have rolled over

[1] Cott. MS., Faustina, c. vii., fol. 125; translated in Foxe's *Acts and Monuments*, iii. 57.   [2] Lechler's *Wiclif*, p. 355.

the land since that day when John Wycliffe went
home to take his wages, it is well that each of us
should ask what he is doing to forward Wycliffe's
work, and what hope he has to share in his reward.
The stream flows further than ever all around the
habitable globe ; is it to be dried up in that England
which Wycliffe loved so well ?   The fire burns clearly
all over the known world ; in the land of John
Wycliffe and Hugh Latimer shall the candle be put
out ?   If not, we must arm for the fight, for the
catastrophe is sorely threatened.   Let us hear what
Wycliffe says to us from beyond the grave, as to the
responsibility of every single soul in Christ's forces.

"And so each member of Christ should have his
proper deed ; but all their deeds should come to this,
that they profit to the body of the Church ; and then
they profit to each member, and to worship Jesus
Christ.   And thus each man should beware that he
is in such a state as is approved by Jesus Christ, and
labour truly in this state.   If thou be a priest of
Christ, teach truly God's law ; if thou be a worldly
lord, defend God's law by strength ; and if thou be
a labourer, keep thou truth and labour diligently.
And thus each man of Christ's Church should help
his brother after his might ; and if he could help
many, he should be many limbs to Him." [1]

And let every man and woman, aye, and child,
among us say, with our hand upon the sword of the
Spirit, in the grand words of Wycliffe's grandest
follower : "Here I stand.   I can do no other.   God
help me !   Amen."

[1] Arnold's *English Works*, ii. 246.

CHAPTER VIII.

THE WRITINGS AND OPINIONS OF WYCLIFFE.

NTIL very lately it was not possible to form any judgment of the opinions of Wycliffe apart from his theses, except at second-hand. His writings were locked up in comparatively inaccessible places,—the great majority of the polemical writings, for instance, are in the Imperial Library of Vienna or the University Library of Prague,—and they were still more hidden from ordinary eyes by the caligraphy, or rather cacography, wherein they were written, which even persons accustomed to reading old manuscripts found it no easy task to decipher. Within the last few years much of this reproach to English students has been removed ; but we must in honesty and humility recognize that Germans as well as Englishmen have shared the work ; nay, to say the least, it is a question if the Germans have not taken the hardest part. The English sermons are scattered in many places, some in the British Museum, some in University and College Libraries, and some in various private collections. In point of date these English sermons stand between the earlier and later divisions of the Latin works.

The majority were evidently written for the use of Wycliffe's itinerant priests, since they are rather expositions than sermons, are much too short to have been preached as they stand, and an occasional hint that the priest may enlarge upon this or that, shows that they were meant rather as specimens and models than as finished works. There are some longer and more elaborate, which may very possibly have been preached in Lutterworth Church.

Let us now inquire, with the help of these writings, what Wycliffe's opinions were on the burning questions of his day,—and where we can gather them, on those of our own,—and how far he was that model Protestant which our Ritualistic neighbours are so anxious to assure us that he was not.

On the subject of monachism, in all its branches, he gives forth no uncertain sound. He simply and utterly hated it in every form. He is hardly prepared even to allow that a friar can by any possibility be a Christian man, or a good man in any sense of the word. "Stinking Orders, . . . who love more their idle muck than they do their brethren in God," "hypocrites," "blind," "full of heresy," "limbs of the fiend," "tattered clouts," "live devils," these are merely a selection from the epithets hurled by the Reformer at the monks. The Order of Christ, he argues, which all Christian men enter at baptism, the rule of Christ, by which all that call Him Lord ought to govern their lives, should be enough for His servants without any new Orders of man's invention. Look in the Scriptures for any word of Christ's to justify the founding of these Orders, and you will discover only one passage—" I know you not!" The worldliness and the avarice of these friars are the points which chiefly annoy him. "They will sit with lords and ladies at the meat full dignely, and in churches they have their places before all other men, so that they cannot be more nigh to worldly state than they be. And everywhere they will be great among the commons, and be called Masters and Doctors for the highness of their name. . . And in this sin abbots and other prelates of the Church."[1]

Upon their covetousness he is equally severe. "They pass Iscariot in avarice and worldly goods."[2] "New Orders beguile the people, both beggars and possessioners,[3] in that they feign them holy to spoil them of worldly goods."[4]

It has been questioned whether Wycliffe styled the Pope Antichrist. Undoubtedly he did, but not in the sense of regarding the Papacy, or the individual Pope, as the Antichrist of the last days exclusively. To him, that is Antichrist which is in opposition to Christ; therefore there are many Antichrists. Whenever, and in so far as, the Pope does this, then and to that extent he becomes identified with Antichrist. In this sense he perpetually terms priests and prelates "limbs of Antichrist." If prelates "judge against the judgment of God, they be

---

[1] Arnold's *English Works*, ii. 62.   [2] *Ibid.*, i. 308.
[3] Both the mendicants and the endowed monks.
[4] *Arnold*, ii. 14.

Antichrists."[1] "Antichrist deigneth not to allege God's law for his power ; but he saith that if men deny it they shall be cursed, slain, and burnt."[2] " He is Antichrist that putteth many thousand lives for his own foul life ; "[3] clearly this refers to the Crusade, which Wycliffe so unsparingly denounced. Again, " Christ taught not to His shepherds to raise up a crusade and kill His sheep with His lambs, and spoil them of their goods ; but this is lore of Antichrist that the fiend hath now brought in, and by this it is known that these be not Peter's vicars."[4] " This word (Matt. v. 11) comforteth men to stand against Antichrist, for he will fast curse men and pursue them as heretics."[5] In one of his longer discourses he says, " Freedom is much coveted, as men know by nature ; but more should this better [*i. e.* spiritual] freedom be coveted of Christian men. But it is known that Antichrist hath more enslaved now the Church than it was under the old law, when they might not bear that service. And Antichrist maketh now new laws, and groundeth them not on God and man. For more ceremonies be now brought in than were in the old law, and [they] more tarry [hinder] men to come to Heaven than did in the old law traditions that were founded by scribes and Pharisees. And one root of this thraldom is the lordship that Antichrist hath ; for he challengeth to be full lord, both ghostly and temporal, and so he tarrieth Christian men to serve Christ in His freedom. So that

---

[1] Arnold's *Select English Works of Wyclif,* ii. 231.
[2] *Ibid.,* i. 111.   [3] *Ibid.,* i. 231.   [4] *Ibid.,* i. 367.   [5] *Ibid.,* i. 412.

Christian men may say, as the poet saith in proverb, 'The frog said to the harrow, Cursed be so many lords.' Now Christian men be chulled,[1] now with popes, and now with bishops, now with cardinals of popes, now with prelates under bishops ; and now they cobble their shoes with censures, as who should chulle a football. But certainly [John the] Baptist was not worthy to loose the thong of Christ's shoe ; and more, Antichrist hath no power to let the freedom that Christ hath brought. Christ gave His freedom to men to come easily to bliss of Heaven, but Antichrist chulleth men, to yield them to give him money. . . . But ever these hypocrites dread that God's law should be showed, and they convict of falsehood, for God and His law be more strong. These hypocrites may for a time hold men in the fiend's thraldom, and feign that they give leave to sin, or gab[2] on God, which is worse, that it is needful to obey thus."[3] "Certes," cries the indignant Reformer, treating elsewhere of the same point, "a fiend of Hell should shame to deceive men by such a skill ! "[4]

On the supreme authority of Holy Writ, Wycliffe speaks very decidedly. Antichrist " passeth the folly of the fiend," because while the devil quoted Scripture when he tempted Christ, the Pope sets up his own law above Scripture.[5] "Antichrist has brought [in]

---

[1] Bandied about, thrown from hand to hand.
[2] To *gab* is to jest deceitfully, to tell falsehoods in sport. Wycliffe often uses the word in the sense of wilfully misrepresenting a person named.
[3] Arnold's *English Works*, ii. 279. [4] *Ibid.*, ii. 254.
[5] *Ibid.*, i. 111.

a law that hindereth the use of God's law, yet the truth of God's law and the debt to use it last evermore and bind men full hard. And it is not light to unbind one of God's commands." [1] " Though there be many truths and divers maxims in the Gospel, nevertheless each of these truths is the substance of God Himself." [2] " Make we not blind men our judges, but learn we wit of God's law." [3] "And thus of all the heretics that Antichrist brought ever in, these that babble to lords, and say that they should not know nor hear the Gospel of Christ, for the clergy should teach them [how] to live, are most perilous in the Church, and most to be shunned as Antichrist." [4]

It was from this principle of the supreme authority and perfect sufficiency of God's word, constantly insisted on in all his preaching and writing, that Wycliffe earned his epithet of " The Evangelical Doctor," by which his Bohemian disciples seem to have known him almost better than by his name.

On the other hand, he has no regard for laws and decretals, traditions, or any addition to Scripture of man's making. " Certainly, as traditions made beside God's law, by priests and by scribes and by Pharisees, blinded them to God's law and made it despised, so it is now [in respect] of God's law by new men's laws, as decretals and decrees. And the Sixth,[5] with Clementines,[6] do much harm to God's law, and enfeeble

[1] Arnold's *English Works*, i. 271.

[2] *Ibid.*, i. 332.   [3] *Ibid.*, ii. 49.   [4] *Ibid.*, ii. 245.

[5] The Sixth Book of the Decretals, issued by Boniface VIII. in 1297, sixty-four years later than the other five.

[6] A further supplement, published 1312—1316.

faith. And thus do these new rules of these three Orders, so that they harm realms and countries that they dwell in. But remedy against this is used by many men, to despise all these laws when they are alleged, and say unto men that allege them that falsehood is [the] more suspected for witness of such laws, since God's law telleth all truth that is needful to men." [1] " Men do worse now [than the Pharisees], for instead of phylacteries men make great volumes of new laws that be not God's commandments." [2]

For "the power of the keys" our Reformer has no respect at all. Listen to him. " They [the bishops] give leave to these friars to preach, . . and Antichrist hath founded a law that these prelates should give such leave, and hath ordained that no parson shall have [a] cure but by his leave. And thus, since many [of] Antichrist's priests be fiends, as was Judas, he hath ordained that such curates should be confirmed of the fiend. . . But what true man would not have horror that priests should not serve their God unless the fiend gave them leave? In the highest work that God hath bidden, the people should let His law to reign, and priests should preach without the Church. But here it is a skilful [3] thing, if pseudo-priests preach amiss, that bishops let them to preach ; but error should be first known, for God's work should not be hindered for [any] thing that men suppose to fall. For then no man should say his prayers, and friars' preaching

---

[1] Arnold's *English Works*, i. 205.   [2] *Ibid.*, ii. 61.
[3] Surprising.

should be suspended, for it is known that they err in these four things that we have said. And bishops should stop all these four, and maintain Christ's ordinance ; for else they show with whom they be, and that the fiend is their father." [1]

Wycliffe's reasoning, as this specimen will show, is not always easy to follow. It is the more difficult here, since " let " in his day had the double meaning of give leave and hinder. In the sentence where it is first used, it seems to have the former meaning, and in the second the latter. The " four things " are also puzzling, since he has mentioned no monkish errors in this sermon except simony and begging. Possibly the reference is to the four Orders.

In another sermon he says, " Thus should prelates beware to grant nothing in the name of God unless they were sure before that God's justice granted it, and this might they not know unless they had [a] revelation ; and if our prelates waited ever [for] such revelation, they should deceive few men or none in granting of such pardons ; but as Peter held his peace in granting of such things, so should they hold their peace, since they be less worthy than Peter, and the common people should not believe them in such cases." [2] Again he cries indignantly, that these popes and prelates " sit in God's Temple, and say they be Christ's vicars, and have more power than even Christ had. For Christ had no power to grant such absolution " as Wycliffe has been speaking of, namely, that

---

[1] Arnold's *English Works*, ii. 173.   [2] *Ibid.*, i. 189.

every man killed in the Crusade, irrespective of
character, should go straight to Heaven,—"and
live on such manner as these popes do. And so
in many points these popes feign that they surpass
in power our Lord Jesus Christ."[1] "The Pope . .
feigneth that these keys be powers, both upon
clergymen and also upon laymen ; power of jurisdiction, and power to absolve and bind. . . These
feigned powers may not be proved, nor perceived
indeed ; and therefore be they feigned, and by craft
of hypocrites is the folk beguiled. And thus true
men say here that there be two keys ; the first is
key of knowledge, and the other key of power.
These keys had Peter and many other apostles,
but Peter had precedence before his other brethren.
This knowledge was not speculative, of geometry
or other sciences, but practical, . . how men should
live by God's law. And after this knowledge came
power to bind and unbind ; and to whom God
granteth the first He granteth the second. And
[the] unity of these keys was not exclusively given
to Peter, since Heaven was open to other folk in
countries that Peter came not in, by keys that Christ
gave to other apostles. And so these feigned keys
be keys of Hell, if they open Hell gates to children
of pride ; and if this Pope have knowledge for
this work, he is master of these keys. For God
will give knowledge to teach His way to Heaven
to whomsoever He likes ; and he is Peter's vicar,

---

[1] Arnold's *English Works*, i. 230.

although neither fiends nor cardinals put him in his throne." [1]

"These keys had Peter with many other saints, for all men that come to Heaven have these keys of God." [2] "Christ sent His disciples to preach generally to the people, without letter or asking of leave of St. Peter. . . . From the time that Paul was converted, three years after, he preached fast, and asked no leave of Peter thereto, for he had leave of Jesus Christ." [3]

Truly our Reformer is a model Protestant in respect to Apostolical succession!

Concerning the royal supremacy, or the question of Church and State, Wycliffe's teaching concurs with that of the reformed Church of England. " The Court should teach men belief, the which is grounded on Christ's order. . . . Thus should realms stop first-fruits, and advancing of cardinals, with other spoilings of this [Roman ?] Court, by the which realms and people be burdened." [4] " And not only such priests have keeping of Christ's Church, but kings and princes of this world, as Isidore [Bishop of Seville] beareth witness. And so each man that God giveth power and wit for to know His will, should after their power and wit profit Christ's Church ; for God will [require] this strictly at doomsday of all such men. For God hath given these men such power to serve God thus in earth." [5] " Lords should rule Christ's Church," and therefore when bishops and priests fail in their duty, they should " be put out of their office

---

[1] Arnold's *English Works*, i. 241.   [2] *Ibid.*, i. 349.
[3] *Ibid.*, i. 176.   [4] *Ibid.*, i. 248.   [5] *Ibid.*, i. 265.

and defiled by other men: thus the wise King
Solomon treated the high priest of his father."¹
"And if this epistle of Paul were fully executed as it
should [be], the realm of England should be dis-
charged [rid] of these four sects that be spoken of; and
then might the realm spend many hundred thousand
marks² more than it spendeth now, if these sects were
expelled. . . . And thus it falleth [to] kings to do, by
the office that God hath given them."³ "And thus
should popes be subject to kings, for thus were both
Christ and Peter. . . . And thus, since the King is
God's vicar, dread ye God in His vicar, and do ye
honour to the King, for love of God whose vicar he is."⁴

"And so Christ denied here (John xix. 36) that He
was secular King of [the] Jews; and so Christ's
clergy should shame to be such lords by title of
Christ; and this should the Pope know, and flee
blasphemy of his Master."⁵ "The Gospel telleth
how one prayed Christ to part the heritage betwixt
him and his brother, but Christ forsook this, and said,
Man, who made Me judge over you? . . And thus if
Christ left to judge betwixt two men of worldly
goods, His vicar should leave to judge all this world."⁶

On another point akin to this—the headship of
Christ over His Church—Wycliffe is as decided
as any Covenanter. "True men say that as long
as Christ is in Heaven, the Church hath the best
Pope, Christ, that is head of all saints. And distance

¹ Arnold's *English Works*, i. 268.   ² A mark was 13*s*. 4*d*.
³ *Arnold*, ii. 269.   ⁴ *Ibid.*, ii. 296.
⁵ *Ibid.*, ii. 124.   ⁶ *Ibid.*, ii. 418.

M

more or less hindereth not Christ to do His deeds,
for He promiseth that He is with His, all days, to
the end of the world. . . We dare not put two
heads, lest the Church were monstrous. . . Each
apostle had in his country full power by help of
Christ, so that none had need of Peter, to run and
be sanctioned by him. . . And so Peter was not
head of the Church, but a captain of the Church ;
and surely warriors will scorn this notion, that if
a man be captain, he is head. Peter was captain
for a time, and after him was Paul captain ; and
there was no strife in this, which of them should be
captain." [1]

Indulgences Wycliffe denounces in no measured
terms, and he regards them, like modern Protestants,
as licences to sin. Beyond this, he considers them
an invasion of the prerogative of God, both as
issuing forgiveness where it cannot be known certainly
that God has forgiven, and as arrogating prescience
to the Pope, who does not know when the day of
judgment is to be, and cannot therefore grant remission of penalty for any given time. He styles this
"a manifest lie, and the abomination of desolation." [2]
" The fiend dreadeth not to feign absolutions and
indulgences, with other gifts that God granted never,
to spoil men of their money, and not for soul heal ;
for then would they give freely these gifts, as Christ
gave Himself and bade others do." [3]   " But man may

[1] Arnold's *English Works*, ii. 412.
[2] Cruciata, *Polemical Works*, Wyclif Society, ii. 592.
[3] Arnold's *English Works*, i. 58.

spend all that he hath about other physicians,[1] and
get him absolutions, yea, after the day of doom, and
many indulgences, with letters of fraternity, that
behoveth him to come to Heaven as soon as he is
dead, and yet may the flux of blood run with all
this, and he may be deeper in sin with all his
dispensations."[2] The Reformer considered dispensations quite unnecessary in order to release a man
from the performance of a wrong or foolish vow.
" If a man vow a thing, and he find after that it were
better to leave it [undone], then he shall leave it, and
have sorrow of his folly beside, but him needeth not
to go to Rome to perform his medeful[3] deed. And
here many be deceived by the power of their rulers ;
they ween that they need to have leave of them to do
as they should do ! "[4] " For else might he [the
Pope] grant pardon for long after the day of doom to
men that God would have damned, for a new-found
prayer, and exalt it for man's love more than the
Paternoster : as men say that a pope hath granted
two thousand years to each man that is contrite, and
confessed of his sin, that saith this orison, ' *Domine
Jesu Christe,*' between the consecration of the mass
and the third ' *Agnus Dei.*' And then it were idle to
travel [*i. e.* on pilgrimage] for any pardon, since a
man might at home get him forty thousand years by
noon ! "[5] " First, they begin with this, that he [the
Pope] is head of Holy Church ; and of this they bring

---

[1] Mark v. 26.   [2] *Arnold,* i. 60.
[3] Deserved, whether in the sense of necessary or of meri-
torious.   [4] *Arnold,* i. 81.   [5] *Ibid.,* i. 137.

forth more — that God must share with him His
treasure; and whereas God hath ordained to hide
whether men shall be saved or damned, these hypocrites say they know well, for they be head of Holy
Church, and then they shall be saved, and know
God's secrets, which man He will have saved, and how
long this [man] shall be in pain. And so he knows
by God's lore when the day of doom shall be, for he
may not for shame grant pardon after the day of
doom ; for after this day be but two places in which
pardon may be feigned, and in neither may such
prelates' pardon profit to men that there be. And
when they grant many thousand winters of such
pardon, either they know that this time shall be
before this day, or else this pardon shall serve for
nought."[1]   " Who dare put on Peter this sin, that he
was negligent in this—that he spared God's treasure,
by which popes profit wisely now ?"[2]   " And patch-
ing this word ' Mary' to the greeting of the angel is
not worth much pardon, though it be two thousand
years, as men say the Pope hath granted for the
saying of an orison betwixt the consecration and
' *Agnus Dei.*'"[3]

Let us now inquire the Reformer's views on confession and absolution.

" ' Whether were easier, to say, Thy sins be forgiven
thee, or else to say, Rise and go ?' as if Christ would
mean this argument: He that hath power to do that
one, hath power to do them both. . . But here men
doubt of the letter, whether priests may forgive sin ;

[1] Arnold's *English Works,* i. 222.   [2] *Ibid.,* i. 238.   [3] *Ibid.,* i. 354.

and it seemeth that they may, for priests may absolve
from sin, and it is all one to absolve men from sin and
to forgive the same sin. And it seemeth that priests
may not forgive sins unto men, for there is no sin here
but if it be offence against God ; but no man may
forgive this but God Himself. And so it seemeth that
our prelates may not here forgive sin. So it is that
men may here forgive trespass done to them, and
remit man's injury as much as in them is, but not
remit utterly sin done against God. (Our Reformer
seems here to be stating both sides of the case, having
done which, he gives his own judgment.) . . Priests
may absolve from sin if they accord with [the] keys
of Christ ; and if they discord from these keys, they
feign them falsely to absolve. And so on two manners
may men be absolved of their sins : and first principally[1] of God, when God's injury is forgiven ; and the
second is absolution by a turn that priests have ; and
if this absolving be true, they keep the bounds that
God gave them, and this absolving have priests as
vicars of God's will. And here lie many deceits in
such absolution, for if this absolving be true, it must
accord with Christ's absolving, and to such absolving
is needful both knowledge and power. . . And so
remission is complete that pertaineth only to God,

[1] An important word, which it is necessary to remember was
not used by Wycliffe in the modern sense of *mainly*, but in the
older signification of a thing being *of the highest quality.* Some
of his arguments will be misunderstood if this word be taken in
its present sense. In a letter written in 1539 we read that the
furs under consideration were " very good, but they shall not be
principal," namely, not of the best quality.

or else remission incomplete that men should have generally, for else Christ would not teach men to pray on this manner,—' Forgive us, Lord, our debts of sin, as we forgive our debtors.' If any man will tell more plainly this sentence by God's law, I will meekly assent thereto, if they prove that they say ; and if any man prove this false or against God's law that I have said now here, I will revoke it meekly. But well I mark this Gospel saith that God gave *such* power to men, but this Gospel saith not that God gave *this* power to men." [1]

This is a most interesting passage. It shows us our Reformer struggling up towards the light, and conscious of the struggle, yet not quite able to rid himself of every link of the old fetters. But let us hear also how he speaks a little later, when the limbs are more free from the shackles.

" Here we should understand that confession that Christ nameth here (Matt. x. 32) is not whispering in the priest's ear, to tell him sin that we have done, but it is granting of truth, the which is openly said, with readiness to suffer therefore." [2]

" By the sentence of the Gospel, if man have full sorrow for his sin, if he speak not after one word, but do well and leave to sin, God forgiveth his sin, as He forgave this woman's sin (Luke vii. 36). And neither Gospel nor reason may contradict this sentence. And so the Pope has new-founded a whispering shrift, and bidden it strictly ; and this shrift doeth sometime good, and also much harm in the Church ; for by

---

[1] Arnold's *English Works*, i. 47.   [2] *Ibid.*, i. 196.

this have prelates men underfoot, and spoil them of worldly goods. And thus both priests and their subjects sin many ways in this point. And thus men err in belief, both priests and the people. For a hundred points be feigned of absolving and cursing that have no ground in God's law, and yet men dare not contradict them. And from the time that the fiend was unbounden, the third Pope Innocent brought this in. And since this doeth much good to many men to be thus shriven, and to many it doeth harm,—and thereof they themselves should be judges,—men say that it is needful to many men to be thus shriven, but when and to whom men should be shriven is in their own discretion. . . And it seemeth hard that the Church should be nourished with new food, and leave freedom that Christ hath ordained, and be constrained to take this food. Shrive a man him well to God : this sufficeth a man to soul's health. And yet it is needful that some men should shrive them thus." [1]

The fetters are not quite got rid of, but the light is coming nearer. At last it has come.

" For God's law speaketh not but of shrift made to God, and of general shrift to men, and to stir them to leave their sin ; and these shrifts be oft better for this than these new whisperings. Here men say, if they durst, that no shrift that now is used is good to man, but inasmuch as it hindereth man from sin. And so, if priests preached diligently, as Christ hath ordained them to preach, it seemeth that this were enough,

[1] Arnold's *English Works*, ii. 206.

with general confession. And so, even if it do good, nevertheless it doth much harm, for confessors have their means to spoil the people by simony, and to foul them many ways." [1]

Wycliffe's conception of the nature of sin was that of Augustine, which has been maintained in our own day by "Rabbi" Duncan—namely, that it is not positive, but privative; not an act so much as a defect; a non-being instead of a being. Augustine was led to this conclusion by his struggle with the Manichees, who maintained the existence of an independent eternal evil principle, opposed to God ; and to the metaphysical minds of Wycliffe and Dr. Duncan it was evidently attractive.

The distinction of the schoolmen between mortal and venial sins Wycliffe regards as dangerous and misleading. "True men say that they know not in this life with revelation which is venial and which is deadly; and these terms, venial and deadly, are found by new men without authority of holy writ, and therefore are [to be] suspected." A little drily our Reformer adds that "it accordeth most with holy writ, reason, and propriety of wording, that this sin is deadly for which a man shall be damned in Hell, and all others be venial." [2]   In which case it necessarily follows that no venial sins exist.

The sin against the Holy Ghost he understood as determined unbelief, and unwillingness to turn to God, persisted in to the end of life. [3]

---

[1] Arnold's *English Works*, ii. 87.
[2] *Ibid.*, iii. 452.   [3] *Ibid.*, ii. 32 ; iii. 120.

We come now to the great question of transubstantiation, upon which pages, almost volumes,
might be filled with extracts from Wycliffe's writings.
He has been accused of holding the Lutheran doctrine of consubstantiation. Let us inquire how far
this is true. There are three main views of the
question, what change, if any, is effected by the words
of consecration. The view commonly called transubstantiation, which as we have seen never existed
before the year 787, is that when the priest has
pronounced the words, " This is My body," the bread
and wine become actually changed into the body
and blood of Christ, so that there is no more the
substance of bread or of wine left. This is what
Wycliffe terms "an accident without a subject"; for
how can the sight, smell, taste, and touch of bread
and wine be left, if the bread and wine themselves
are gone ? Against this view he warred with all the
energy that was in him. With scathing satire he
inquires if a man can be drunk through a logical
"accident"?[1] "It is kindly [*i. e.* by nature] bread,
as Paul saith,[2] but it is sacramentally verily God's
body. And therefore saith Austin, 'That thing is
bread that thine eyes tell thee, and that thou seest
with them.' For it was not supposed before the fiend
was loosed, that this worthy sacrament was accident
without subject. And yet dwell true men in the old

---

[1] Arnold's *English Works*, i. 361.
[2] 1 Cor. x. 17 ; xi. 26.—Wycliffe's Roman Catholic editor,
Mr. Arnold, "does not know to what passage the writer
refers" !

belief, and lately, friars foul themselves in their new heresy."[1]

Certainly Wycliffe did not hold *trans*ubstantiation, his enemies themselves being judges. Did he then, as Mr. Arnold takes pains to show, hold *con*substantiation—namely, that the bread and wine remain, but that there is along with them a certain mysterious and corporeal presence, by which the body of Christ is truly and physically eaten? Did he, in the second place, hold a half-way view, that there is a presence, apart from the faith of the recipient, of a supernatural kind, yet spiritual and not corporeal? Or did he hold the opinion of Berenger before him, and of Zuingle after him—that the bread is eaten with the mouth, and the body of Christ with the soul alone; that there is no presence whatever in the elements, but only the sign, emblem, and remembrance of Christ? He certainly opposed the view of some, that the sacrament was "nought";[2] but in using these words he appears to be merely making sarcastic allusion to the "accident without subject," which he hints is equivalent to nothing. Dr. Lechler is of opinion that Wycliffe's view was the second of the three above mentioned, namely, half-way between Luther and Zuingle; and Professor Burrows pronounces it "neither Lutheranism, nor Calvinism, nor Zuinglianism. It neither denies the presence nor explains the mode." It was, in fact, as the Professor observes, exactly the doctrine of the Church of England—namely, that "the body of Christ is given,

---

[1] Arnold's *English Works*, i. 133.   [2] *Ibid.*, ii. 386, 421.

taken, and eaten, in the supper, *only* after a heavenly and spiritual manner,"[1] and that "the sacramental bread and wine remain still in their very natural substances, and therefore may not be adored, for that were idolatry to be abhorred of all faithful Christians; and the natural body and blood of our Saviour Christ are in Heaven, and not here."[2] One passage only seems to contradict this conclusion—in his Latin tract *De Apostasia Cleri*, wherein he says that "those who deny that the bread which is the sacrament is the body of Christ, fall into the error of Berenger, . . which is against the faith of Scripture and the four great doctors."[3] Apart from this, as to what he really held, let Wycliffe speak, and let my readers judge.

"Right so the sacred host is very bread kindly, and God's body figuratively."[4] "The sacred host, that is in figure Christ's body."[5] Wycliffe does not believe that the sixth chapter of John contains any distinct and intentional reference to the sacrament. "Christ speaketh not yet of the sacred host, since

[1] Article xxviii.

[2] The "black rubric" at the end of the Communion Service: this rubric was written by John Knox.

[3] Lechler's *Wyclif*, p. 386, Latin original 397.—I have no means of ascertaining the date of this tract. Some of these Latin tracts are much earlier than the English sermons, and Wycliffe might have written disparagingly, say in 1370, of an opinion which he held warmly in 1382. It is by his latest language only that this point can be decided. The passage quoted from Ralph Higden (p. 100) shows that Wycliffe's enemies identified his view with that of Berenger. See also his theses, p. 101.

[4] Arnold's *English Works*, ii. 6.   [5] *Ibid.*, ii. 73.

on Shrove Thursday He ordained it." [1] Nevertheless
" many of these words may be well understood of
this sacred host." But if the consecrated bread be
not eaten " ghostly," namely, spiritually and by faith,
" men take not worthily the sacrament more than
a beast. . . This host is eaten bodily and ghostly of
some men, but Christ's body in his kind is not eaten
bodily. . . But ever wit we that this host is very
bread in his kind, and in figure God's body, by virtue
of Christ's words ; but thus it is not of Christ's flesh
and His blood in his kind." [2]

"This host is bread in his kind," he writes again,
" as be other unconsecrated hosts, and sacramentally
God's body ; for Christ saith so, that may not lie.
And so, if this sacrament be fouled in that that it is
bread or wine, it may not thus be defiled in things
which it figureth.   And so a man breaketh not God's
body, nor drinketh His blood with his mouth, although
he eat and drink the bread and the wine that are
these [things] ; for they be not these by nature, as
[John the] Baptist was not by nature Elijah.   And
thus a mouse eateth not Christ's body, although it
eat this sacrament ; for the mouse faileth ghostly
wit." [3] " So men eat the sacred host to eat Christ
ghostly, *that is, have mind of Him*, how kindly He
suffered for man.   And such a fruitful remembrance
of Christ is ghostly meat to the soul, and ghostly
eating of Christ's body, that the Gospel of John
speaketh of." [4]

[1] Arnold's *English Works*, ii. 81.   [2] *Ibid.*, ii. 112.
        [3] *Ibid.*, ii. 169.   [4] *Ibid.*, ii. 287.

Verily, this man taught no consubstantiation! Neither did he enjoin fasting communion. He says, Christ "gave the sacrament to them [the apostles] after their meat commonly, and Christ spake with them commonly after that they had somewhat eaten. . . And since taking of this thing [food] 'in measure was no sin in Christ's time, what virtue hath man's statute to make this be sin more than then? These foolish words do away with Christ's freedom, and belief that men should have. If this be no sin to God, it is no sin for to charge to eat in measure before the mass, and after to sing and use." [1]

In the same manner Wycliffe speaks of baptism. "Baptizing is a figure how men's souls should be baptized from sin. . . Baptizing is a token of washing of the soul from sin, both original and actual, by power taken by Christ's death." [2] Distinctly he says, "God is not so restricted to sensible sacraments that He may not without them give a man His grace." In the case of the Innocents, Wycliffe believed that "as God gave martyrs grace, without baptism of water, by baptism of the Holy Ghost and by water of Christ's side, so may men suppose of circumcision ; and so all these innocents were circumcised in soul." [3] Infant baptism he admitted and approved.[4] But he evidently did not believe in baptismal regeneration as a necessary accompaniment of this sacrament.

Let us consider next the interesting questions of

[1] Arnold's *English Works*, i. 361.
[2] *Ibid.*, ii. 328.   [3] *Ibid.*, ii. 329.
[4] *Ibid.*, ii. 328 ; *Lechler*, p. 373.

the invocation of saints, image-worship, and Mariolatry. Compared with the amount which he has
to say about the mendicant friars, indulgences, and
the Papacy, our Reformer is strangely silent on these
far more vital points. Indeed, it seems to be only
at the very close of his life that he took these
questions into any serious consideration. In his
earlier sermons he is silent about the whole matter
of saint-worship ; but when he does speak, we find
that he retained the ideas originally instilled into
him. In the sermons on the Gospels and Epistles,
the work of his later years, he does just allude to
the question in two passages, which show that his
mind has been slightly awakened to the uselessness
of image-worship ; but that the sin of idolatry is
involved in it does not even yet seem to have
entered his head. " Men that go to church and
kiss pillars, and hear afterwards many masses,
and have with this an unclean heart, eat nor or
evilly God's body," he writes in one sermon.[1] And
in another, "If these feasts, with these images and
these hours, were left [alone] by men, and then
they loved better Christ, and did better service
that He bade them, then it would be profitable
to such men to leave such ceremonies. And it
seemeth to many men, since Christ, with all His
apostles, left all such things, and lived better in
charity, and kept better the bidding of God, so
men might now do."[2]

Wycliffe very lightly valued Papal canonizations.

---

[1] Arnold's *English Works*, ii. 170.   [2] *Ibid.*, i. 330.

"It is true that many be saints in Heaven, as Lawrence and Katherine, although Rome canonize them never." He thought also that much harm came by "the purchasing of canonizing of saints at Rome."[1]

But when he comes to write "The Ten Commandments" he uses very different language. "And so in trust of images many are deceived, in hope of help or health in any sort of need, as the old law and the new witness." He then proceeds to quote Acts xvii. 24—29.[2] In his Latin "Book of the Commandments" he is even more explicit. "The effect of every image should only be this, to wake up the mind and heart of a man to attend to heavenly things; but when this effect has been produced, the sooner the imagination of the man drops all attention to the qualities of the image, so much the better, for in the continued dwelling of the imagination upon these qualities lies concealed the venom of idolatry. As now the first and greatest commandment forbids us to pray to any work of man, insomuch that it was prohibited to the Jews to make any images whatsoever, it is manifest that it behoves us to take the greatest care to be on our guard against the poison under the honey. . . The people, therefore, must be faithfully warned of the danger which lies in this matter, especially as merely nominal Christians, men of an animal nature, dismissing all faith in spiritual things, are wont at the present day to feed their senses to excess in religion—as their

---

[1] Arnold's *English Works*, i. 330.   [2] *Ibid.*, iii. 83.

eyes with the sumptuous spectacle of the Church's ornaments, their ears with bells, and organs, and the new art of striking the hour of the day by the wonderful chimes, not to mention many other sensuous preparations by which their other senses are moved, apart altogether from religious feeling." [1] Is the warning quite unneeded in this present day? The subject of Mariolatry appears to be that on which Wycliffe's mind was slowest in awakening to the truth. In his early sermons he teaches without the least apparent misgiving what Romanists term " the Catholic view of Mary "—that view which to Protestant eyes sets her usually beside, and sometimes above, the God whose creature she was. Modern Protestants who do not mix much in Romish society have scarcely an idea of what this view really is. Let it be stated in the words of a living Roman Catholic writer. " God came down to live on earth for three and thirty years. Three years out of that time He gave to the task of redeeming the world, and thirty He gave to Mary. *That was His estimate of her.*" For nearly the whole of his long life, Wycliffe held this view of her whom he terms " the Lady of this world."

In his early work (if it be his) on the " Ave Maria," he writes, " Men greet commonly our Lady, God's Mother, and we suppose that this greeting saveth many men. For we take as belief that she is blessed in Heaven, and Christ will do at her praying among all other saints." A little further on he remarks that

---

[1] Lechler's *Wiclif*, p. 332.

the prayer commonly termed the Angelical Salutation adds two words, " Mary " and " Jesus," to the exact words used by Gabriel: he does not like this, for " men should not upon great penalty add unto God's word." Wherefore " trust we unto words of the Gospel, and worship we Jesus and Mary with all our might." [1]

In his early Latin sermons, also, Wycliffe carries on the same idea. It seems to him " impossible that we should obtain the reward [of eternal life] without the help of Mary. . . For she was herself in some measure the cause of the incarnation and passion of Christ, and so of the whole redemption of the world. There is no sex or age, no rank or position of any one in the whole human race, which has no need to call for the help of the holy Virgin." [2] Several times he tells us that she was sinless,[3] and repeats the favourite Popish idea of her perpetual virginity.[4] " Christ and His mother must needs be of one will," says he ;[5] an assertion which he assuredly did not get from his Bible.[6] After all this Popish rubbish come two or three sermons in which the mind of the preacher seems to have been aroused to misgiving, and the old convictions are struggling with the new.

---

[1] Arnold's *English Works*, iii. 111—113. Too much stress must not be laid on the word *worship*, which in Wycliffe's day was merely equivalent to honour. He speaks in various places of the duty of worshipping the Church, preachers, rulers, &c., evidently meaning only honour.

[2] Lechler's *Wiclif*, p. 333.

[3] Arnold's *English Works*, i. 257, &c.   [4] *Ibid.*, i. 317, &c.

[5] *Ibid.*, i. 353.   [6] Luke ii. 48 ; Mark iii. 21, 31.

This is usually the case in the transition period of a reformer's life, and the illogical consequences are curious to behold. "Some men construe this [Luke ii. 35] thus: that our Lady, by this sorrow, loved more tenderly mankind, and made them show their private sins. And so by this merit[1] of our Lady, thoughts of apostles and others were showed by many hearts to God by confession; or else that our Lady thought more of the deeds that Christ did, and showed them to Luke and others, to witness them in many hearts."[2] Wycliffe evidently read "that the thoughts of many hearts may be revealed" as a sequence to "a sword shall pierce through thine own soul also." In this last-quoted passage there is a scrap of the old leaven; and yet even this, by "some men construe this thus," does not seem quite convincedly adopted as his own opinion. And in the very same sermon he tells us that "Simeon thought that by Him Mary and Joseph could be saved."[4] If Mary were capable of salvation, how could she be sinless?

In another sermon he tells us that Christ "ordained her to be mistress to His apostles," and "the Church singeth of our Lady that she hath destroyed all heretics, for she is special mistress to destroy all heretics." Yet in the sentence immediately before this, we read that "our Lady might not come to bliss unless she had heard and kept His word."[5]

---

[1] By this word Wycliffe usually means moral worth, not merit in the modern sense.　　　　[2] *Arnold*, i. 333.

[3] *Ibid.*, i. 333.　　　[4] *Ibid.*, i. 332.　　　[5] *Ibid.*, p. 380, 381.

He believed also that " Christ showed Himself spiritually to His mother, and told her how He was risen,"
another event which he did not find recorded in his
Bible.

Even to the last Wycliffe cannot shake himself
free from the idea that it is possible to "please our
Lady," and that Christians ought to wish and try
to do so. Had he lived longer, doubtless God would
have given him clearer light. But after all, in his
later sermons he says very little about the Virgin.
In the majority of instances in which she is named,
it is to urge Christians to imitate her purity and
humility.

Purgatory was a place in the existence of which
Wycliffe believed, during the time in which he was
writing his English sermons. It is only when we
come to the latest Latin polemical works that we find
him first expressing doubt of it, and then distinctly
denying it.[1] The evangelical view, therefore, upon
this head, appears to be one of the last convictions
adopted by the Reformer. Comparatively few of the
Lollards had not some faith in Purgatory, which they
showed by leaving bequests for masses to be said
for the repose of their souls. Wycliffe speaks of such
masses, not in a style of strong censure, but in such
a way as to let us perceive that he put very little
faith in their efficacy.

And now we come to the last and most deeply
interesting of the more important section of Wycliffe's
opinions. Did he hold the Lutheran, or rather the

[1] *Polemical Works,* i. 46—48.

N 2

Augustinian, doctrine of justification by faith? The
only answer that can be given is that it never seems
to have dawned upon him in the full light in which
God revealed it to Augustine and to Luther. The
real faith itself was undoubtedly in his heart. But
to the last, like all Papists, he seems unable to detect
any difference between justification and sanctification.
The fetters of the law are ever clanking about him.
Yet no man ever more fully preached the one offering
of Christ as a full and sufficient sacrifice for the sins
of the world. The sufficiency and efficacy of the
cross in which he trusted, he apprehended perfectly
on earth ; the value of the process by which that
sacrifice was apprehended he only learned in Heaven.

CHAPTER IX.

WYCLIFFE'S OPINIONS ON MINOR POINTS.

E come now to Wycliffe's opinions on matters of smaller import.

Next to the mendicant friars, the heaviest vials of the Reformer's wrath are poured out upon endowments. He hates them with deadly hatred. They did not exist in the early Church (he thinks the Jewish Church, as usual, beside the mark) ; Christ and His apostles were not endowed, nor ought the clergy to be so now. " This venom [of pride] came much in from the time that the Church was endowed." [1] " Christ purchased not to His apostles rents, nor houses, nor worldly goods, but taught them both openly and secretly to flee such possessions of the world." [2] " And for dread of loss of these temporalities, they dare not reprove sin of lords and mighty men, nor freely condemn covetousness in worldly men, nor in maintaining of false pleas." [3] At the same time the Reformer strongly exhorts his disciples

[1] Arnold's *English Works*, ii. 31.   [2] *Ibid.*, ii. 290.
[3] *Ibid.*, iii. 215.

to be free in their voluntary offerings to good and worthy priests.[1]

On the question of liturgies and forms of prayer Wycliffe speaks uncertainly, sometimes appearing to commend and sometimes to condemn them. He speaks of monks who " learn their own rule, and leave the rule that God gave, and occupy them in this lore, to say and sing without book, as if this pleased most to God." [2] Again, " Christian men . . . be more bound to learn holy writ, and preach the Gospel, and God's commands, and works of mercy, than to say matins and mass and evensong by Salisbury use." [3] " God forbid that any Christian man [should] understand that this here incensing and crying [intoning [4]] that men use now be the best service of a priest, and most profitable to man's soul. For Jesus Christ and His apostles used it [not], nor charged priests thereto ; but they prayed devoutly and stilly, in nights and hills, and preached the Gospel openly and freely, and died therefore. For, as Austin and Gregory witness, prayer is better done by compunction and weeping and holy desire of righteousness, than by great crying and blowing of man's voice." [5] " Wonder it is," cries our Reformer, " why men praise so much this new praying, with great crying and high song, and leave still manner of praying, as Christ and His apostles did. It seemeth that we seek our own liking

---

[1] Arnold's *English Works*, i. 234, 284, &c.

[2] *Ibid.*, ii. 301. [3] *Ibid.*, iii. 402.

[4] Wycliffe's Roman Catholic editor allows this to be his meaning. [5] Arnold's *English Works*, iii. 403.

and pride in this song more than the devotion and understanding of that that we sing, and this is great sin. . . One paternoster sung with devotion and understanding is better than many thousand sung without devotion and understanding. And this new praying occupieth men so much that they have no space to study holy writ and teach it. But Austin asketh, Who may excuse him from preaching and seeking and saving of souls, for love of contemplation? . . and Gregory saith in his Pastorals, They that have plenty of virtues and knowledge of God's law, and go into [the] desert for [the] rest of contemplation, are guilty of as many souls as they might profit to in knowledge of men dwelling in the world. Wherein shall this new song excuse us from learning and preaching of the Gospel that Christ taught and bade?" [1]

I doubt from the above extracts whether the Evangelical Doctor would have listened to modern parishioners in behalf of what they facetiously call a "hearty" service, but which would more correctly be named an ear-pleasing one.

In respect of Latin services Wycliffe speaks quite as strongly. "By authority of the law of God, men should speak their words as God's law speaketh, and strange not in speech from understanding of the people, and always beware that the people understand well." [2] "One comfort is of knights, that they savour much the Gospel, and have will to read in English the Gospel of Christ's life." [3] "And if

---

[1] Arnold's *English Works*, iii. 228, 229.   [2] *Ibid.*, i. 79.
[3] *Ibid.*, i. 209.

Germans may reasonably defend the use of their own language [in reading the Scriptures], so ought the English reasonably to defend the use of their own tongue." [1]

Some Christians, during times of persecution, have questioned how far it is allowable to avoid it by flight. Wycliffe had no doubt concerning this. "Thus [see Matt. xiv. 13] Christ gave ensample to us to flee death when He moveth us." [2] "And if you ask when men should flee, and when stand in God's cause, certainly sometimes men be constrained to come and to answer for Christ; and so, if we live good life and neglect not the love of Christ, He shall teach us to flee and to answer as we should." [3]

On the point of human merit, Wycliffe commonly uses the English words 'merit' and 'demerit' in the sense of moral worth and moral worthlessness. He distinguishes, like the schoolmen, between merit of condignity, or acts which deserve the favour of God, and merit of congruity, or acts done by the grace of God. Concerning the former he speaks without the least hesitation: "No creature can merit any thing from God by condignity." [4] "I do not believe that even the smallest sin committed against the Lord can be deleted by any merit, unless it is done away in the main by the merit of this Man (Christ)." [5] "I do not see how any sin can be done away with by means of merit of condignity in the sinner, since

---

[1] *Polemical Works,* i. 168.
[2] Arnold's *English Works,* i. 122.   [3] *Ibid.,* i. 207.
[4] Lechler's *Wiclif,* p. 320.   [5] *Ibid.,* p. 314.

infinite grace is required in order to satisfaction for sin."[1] Many of the schoolmen, however, held that man, by an honest, innocent, moral life, could deserve (of congruity) that God should give him converting grace. Wycliffe treats this idea as a vain imagination. Then can man, after conversion, merit Heaven by his good works? Wycliffe replies, Not of condignity; but he admits a certain amount of merit of congruity, a working of man with God, which entitles him to look for the future reward of his good works. Works of supererogation, to be applied to others, he indignantly rejects as a "lying fiction."[2]

Was Wycliffe a Calvinist or an Arminian? Neither. Like most men brought up in Popish error, and afterwards taught from the Bible, he was a curious mixture of the two. He taught predestination in so strong a manner that it verged on fatalism, and he denied universal redemption, holding that Christ died for the elect alone; but he held that no man could possibly know whether he were one of the elect, nor could one man know it of another until it were seen whether he died in the faith. No Roman Catholic, as such, can be a Calvinist, for there is nothing which Rome hates as she hates those doctrines of grace commonly termed Calvinism. One of her chief dignitaries is said to have asserted that there is no sect or body whence Rome has not won a convert except Calvinism.

On the important question of Sabbath-keeping Wycliffe is far in advance of his time, and even of

---

[1] Lechler's *Wiclif*, p. 314.   [2] *Ibid.*, p. 316.

his brother Lollards. To few indeed of them did
it occur that Sunday ought to be kept otherwise than
as all around them kept it—church in the morning,
amusement in the afternoon. Wycliffe, however,
writes that "we should spend the holy day in praising
of God, and else we sin greatly in failing of His
service ; . . . for no feast nor service is pleasing to
God but inasmuch as it sharpeth a man to love our
Lord Jesus Christ. . . . And Christian men should
learn by teaching of priests, and busy them devoutly
on the holy day to study on virtues, and on the ten
commandments, and on the seven deeds of mercy,
bodily and ghostly, and speak with men, and specially
with them of heavenly things, and put away guiles
and wrongs and other sins, and learn we to love God
in perfect charity."[1]

The seven bodily works of mercy here referred
to are—feeding the hungry, giving drink to the
thirsty, harbouring strangers, clothing the naked,
visiting the sick, visiting prisoners, and burying the
dead. The seven ghostly or spiritual works are—
teaching, counselling, chastisement, comforting, for-
giving, endurance, and prayer.

The Rector of Lutterworth was no admirer of
the modern Ritualistic notion that the Church is
identical with the clergy. He held, as we have
already seen, that every Christian is a priest to
God, and has the power of the keys no less than
pope or prelate—more, if the pope and the prelate
are bad men and "limbs of Antichrist." His words

---

[1] Arnold's *English Works*, iii. 85.

are particularly indignant on this point. "And when the King and secular lords perceive well that [the] clergy waste their ancestors' alms in pomp and pride, gluttony, and other vanities, and they would take again the superfluity of temporal goods, and help the land and themselves and their tenants, these worldly clergy cry loud that they be cursed for intermeddling with Holy Church's goods. As if secular lords and the commons were no part of Holy Church, but only proud priests, full of covetousness, simony, and extortions, and all other sins."[1]

Of clerical celibacy he says: "Priests be wifeless against God's authority; for Christ . . . approved wedding in apostles and many other."[2] Yet he never married, nor is one instance known of a Lollard priest venturing to do so. Wycliffe's opinion of women was rather higher than that of most men in his day. He thought them frail articles,[3] yet not therefore to be despised, but to be cared for and to have allowances made for them; and he considered that while a good woman was one of the best things which God had made, a bad one was among the worst things in existence. The popular idea of most men in his time was that a good woman was merely a woman who had never been tempted to evil, and that female virtue of any kind was a poet's dream. Concerning male virtue they were not quite so sceptical. The Reformer is inclined to be less hard on the weaker sex. "Women

---

[1] Arnold's *English Works*, iii. 275.   [2] *Ibid.*, i. 364.
[3] *Ibid.*, ii. 139.

be of short wit," he admits ; " but folly and lusts of men be more often to blame than women."[1]

He is, notwithstanding, very severe on the great ladies of his day, who suffered themselves to be influenced by the friars to move their lords to large donations to monasteries, foundations of chantries, and so forth. " As if women knew not God's law in endowing priests, and it seemeth to women's wit both alms and mercy, and they move lords thereto ; . . this sin is in these proctors,[2] but more in these lords. And thus fiends' wills of friars acquaint them with ladies, and they be means to lords to have that these fiends ask. . . For who may deny that lords do after ladies, or that friars counsel with ladies, or much sin is now up by works of lords ? . . But unknowing of God's law excuseth them not here, for that should lords trow, and not these false means."[3]

Private chaplains and family confessors win little favour in our Reformer's eyes. He evidently looks upon those who covet and strive after such a position as men who love good dinners and easy chairs, high titles and full pay.

But neither does he easily let off the ladies and gentlemen who are of the same mind.

"And if thou be proud of shape that God hath given thee, thou shouldst well know, by wit that He has lent thee, that in each stone or other foul body is as fair shape as any that thou hast. And so such men that boosen [puff out] their breasts,

---

[1] Arnold's *English Works*, i. 389.
[2] That is, the women.   [3] Arnold's *English Works*, i. 389.

or pinch their bellies to make them small waists, or strain their hose to show their strong legs, seem to accuse God of gifts that He has given them, and amend Him in His craft as if He failed therein. And in this pride sin women by making of their puffs, and generally in attire of their body; [so] that commonly, from the head to the foot, men deform their body by their foul attire, as pikes of shoes, and garlands of heads, and tattering of clothes beareth open witness. . . Men should think how God made him in the state of innocence, without any clothing, like angels or beasts; and because of sin this ape made him clothing; and this is no matter of pride but of sorrow." [1]

Ladies are usually considered the fashionable half of mankind, and it will be seen that Wycliffe pours out the larger half of his satire on the gentlemen. He might well do so, for in his day the latter were by far the more extravagant dressers of the two. The piked shoes refers to the long-pointed cracowes, which came in in 1381; and the delicately-cut borders of sleeves, puffings and slashings, are doubt-less what our unæsthetic Reformer intends by "tatter-ing of clothes."

The light in which Wycliffe views amusements would not be popular at the present day. He classed them all under the head of babyish non-sense. "Some men have [a] child's will, who feed their intellects with sensible things and tricks of childish games, as if they were fools, and after this

[1] Arnold's *English Works*, iii. 124.

come to men's wit holding all this folly. But they
give themselves to jousting and archery and wrestling,"—here he names the favourite sport of the
upper, middle, and lower classes respectively,—" and
these follow off more folly than doth the first age."[1]
This appears to mean, that such men are more silly
than little children. Doubtless an extreme view
to take of the matter; yet is the present day quite
innocent of going to an extreme in the opposite
direction? Nor is he more lenient to "playing
at the tables (backgammon), chess, and other vanities."[2] Again he says: "Some men look to vain
plays, and many sights of worldly things, the which
profit not to their soul, but rather do them harm."[3]
In Wycliffe's day there were scarcely any plays but
of the religious order, such as the Ober-Ammergau
Passion Play. What would he have said to the
modern theatre?

Our Reformer is no admirer of dinner-parties.
Enumerating the "works of the flesh," he says, "The
seventeenth sin be eatings together, as early dinners
and late suppers,"—10 a.m. and 4 p.m. were the
usual hours for these meals in his day,—"for these
fall to such [foolish] fellowships, and many unreason-
able words. Many such works come of the flesh
that hinder men from the kingdom of Heaven."[4]

It has been questioned how far the indulgence
of wit and humour, of irony and sarcasm, is compatible with the Christian life. Wycliffe would have

---

[1] Arnold's *English Works*, i. 410.   [2] *Ibid.*, iii. 286.
[3] *Ibid.*, i. 250.   [4] *Ibid.*, ii. 350.

allowed this to the full. He even goes further, and maintains that every man to whom God has given the faculty of satire is bound to use it in His service. "If Christ scorned her [the Canaanitish woman], which I dare not say, scorning was lawful, as holy writ proveth. For Elias the prophet bade the priests of Baal that they should strongly cry, lest their god slept, or spake with other men, [so] that he might not hear them. And thus scorneth Paul, speaking to Corinthians: 'Wherein did I less to you than other apostles did, but that I took not of you? Forgive me this wrong.'[1] And so oft in God's law is scorning well meant, as if it were lawful done on good manner."[2]

In one of his Latin tracts he writes: "If 'He who sitteth in the heavens laughs at them,' so also may all men on God's side bring that school of theologians to shame with raillery, with reproaches, or with proofs, as God has given them severally the ability. . . When any one, from a motive of love to his neighbour, breaks out into words of reproach and scorn, in order to defend God's honour and to preserve the Church from errors, such a man, if uninfluenced by revenge and ambition, does a work worthy of praise."[3]

On costly churches and splendid abbeys ("painted houses" is his term) Wycliffe looked with severe

---

[1] 2 Cor. xii. 13.—The playfulness of St. Paul is so exquisitely delicate that it appears to be imperceptible to most readers.

[2] Arnold's *English Works*, i. 114.

[3] Lechler's *Wiclif*, p. 473.

disapprobation. In many places he speaks sternly of the action of the friars in robbing the poor of their hard-earned money in order to indulge themselves in architectural vain-glory;[1] for he looked with no milder eyes upon the lovely Gothic edifices that rose around him, which our sentimental Ritualistic friends are so fond of attributing to the single-eyed devotedness of those holy monks. "Christ and His apostles made no great churches nor cloisters."[2] "Christ told little [set little value] by the Temple, or any such works of craft that pass the state of innocence; for clean life without such is better to Christ than such churches. All such profit not but inasmuch as they help the people to hear God's word, and better there to pray God; and this is commonly better done in the air under heaven, but oft-time, in rainy weather, churches do good on holy day. And thus curiosity[3] of fools is not founded on God's law."[4] "And thus at the beginning they [friars] feign them most poor of all clergy, but at last they surpass all others in great houses and costly libraries, in great feasts, and many other prides and covetousnesses."[5] He speaks with some disapproval of the consecration of churches and altars, which he termed "japes"[6]—namely, mischievous tricks; but when such offices were done for money, he thunders about simony and filthy lucre. Washing the feet

---

[1] *Polemical Works*, i. 39.
[2] Arnold's *English Works*, iii. 380.
[3] Invention, not inquisitiveness.
[4] Arnold's *English Works*, i. 235.   [5] *Ibid.*, iii. 397.
[6] *Ibid.*, ii. 89.

of the poor on Maundy Thursday he considered "the service of the Church foully turned upside down."[1] "And as to pardons, and holy water, and blessings of bishops, it is a feigned thing for pride of state and covetousness of worldly muck, and to blind the people, and to make them over little to dread sin."[2] Nor did he approve of prelates "calling their friends to fat dignities in the Church."[3]

Pilgrimages came in also for censure. "And if men *foolily* vow to go to Rome or Jerusalem, Canterbury, or other pilgrimages, that we charge more than the great vow made of our christendom [*i. e.* we value it more highly than the vows of our baptism], to keep God's commandments, and forsake the fiend and all his works."[4] He accuses them also of fostering immorality.[5]

"These new fraternities or guilds made of men" do not escape condemnation from our Reformer in that curious document "The Great Sentence of Curse Expounded." "They bring in much pride, vanity, and waste, cost, and trust in men's help more than in God's." Some good Protestants, among others, will scarcely agree with him that "men of subtle craft, as Freemasons and others, seem openly cursed by this sentence."[6]

As regards the existence of ghosts or fairies, our Reformer is strictly non-committal, and declines to decide the point. "Some men dream of these fiends

---

[1] Arnold's *English Works*, ii. 118. [2] *Ibid.*, iii. 453.
[3] *Ibid.*, ii. 152. [4] *Ibid.*, iii. 283. [5] *Ibid.*, i. 83.
[6] *Ibid.*, iii. 333.

that some be elves, and some goblins, and have not
but little power to tempt men in harm of soul. But
since we cannot prove this, nor disprove this speedily,
hold we us in the bonds that God telleth in His
law."[1]   These words sound as if his private opinion
were "rather nay than yea."

His respect for recently-invented saintly legends
was small enough, yet he evidently believed fully
in the older legends—those of St. Margaret, St.
Catherine, and St. Lawrence.[2]

It is a little difficult to define Wycliffe's opinion
upon war, for his utterances in various places are
rather contradictory. Probably, as in so many other
cases, his views developed gradually, and were not
at the close of his life what they had been at an
earlier period. He certainly disliked it at all times ;
yet how far it is fair to say that he thought it wicked
in the abstract, will be best left to the judgment of
those who read the following passages :—

"It is likely that [the] prince of the world is
author of battles that men now use. . . We grant
the fiend that in the Old Testament it was lawful
to fight, as God's law teaches us ; and now in the
new law were lawful to fight if such circumstances
were as were in the old law; and else should men
be in peace, for love of our God. Soothly, in the
old law men fought with God's enemies, to avenge
God's injury, and by none other cause ; and neither
should men now [do otherwise], if their fighting be

---

[1] Arnold's *English Works*, ii. 366.
[2] *Ibid.*, i. 187, 330; iii. 344.

lawful."[1] "And secular lordships, that clerks have full falsely against God's law, and spend them so wickedly, should be given wisely by the King and witty [wise] lords to poor gentlemen that would justly govern the people and maintain the land against enemies; and then might our land be stronger by many thousand men-at-arms than it is now, without any new cost of lords, or talliage [taxation] of the poor commons."[2]

"By this lore may we see how far it is from [the] school of Christ to chide, or to plead, or to fight, as men now do."[3] "Here men think that Christian men should always love peace, and not procure to fight; for Christ is a peaceable King, . . and Christ shall fight for us."[4] "And thus if we lead Christ's life, and believe in Him and in His words, we know well that He bade us not buy swords to fight with them, to slay our brethren bodily, and avenge us on our enemies."[5] "He (Christ) might not fight nor slay, but when He knew that it was just."[6] "And so it seemeth no Gospel deed neither to fight nor prison men, unless God bade to do thus, and then men do as God's servants."[7] "For it is sometimes a work of mercy to deny men worldly goods, and sometimes to take [them] from them, and sometimes to put them in prison, and sometimes to maim them, and sometimes to slay them. And God knows when such deeds profit to man's soul."[8] Our

---

[1] Arnold's *English Works*, iii. 136.   [2] *Ibid.*, iii. 217.
[3] *Ibid.*, i. 17.   [4] *Ibid.*, i. 212.   [5] *Ibid.*, ii. 92.
[6] *Ibid.*, ii. 120.   [7] *Ibid.*, ii. 199.   [8] *Ibid.*, ii. 207.

Reformer evidently is not of opinion that the magistrate or the executioner is a superfluity.

But Wycliffe disliked law quite as much as he disliked war. "And this moveth many men to flee man's judgment, both to be judge and witness, and to plead in this market ; for this manner of judgment followeth too little God's will. And if it follow any time, it falleth as a blind man casteth his staff; for if a man have right to a thing, that right cometh of God to him, and God judgeth that he is worthy to have this thing by His sentence. But what judge in man's plea can know his worthiness? And therefore God forbiddeth this strife ; for both the judge and his consentors do here against the judgment of God."[1]

Wycliffe thought, as many (though not all) good men have done, that intellectual attainments were rather a hindrance to the Christian life. "Christian men should learn God's law, and hold them paid thereby ; and in this measure, and in this number, and in this weight, should they live here, and wait for learning in Heaven that men might have over this. And this learning that Christ taught is enough for this life. And if men live after[2] Him they shall have learning as they have need ; and thus these endowments make learning that doeth harm to Christ's Church, both learning of vanity and thereto learning of men's laws. Christ gave learning the which He loved, that He would teach Christian men ; and other learning and more, over this, would

---

[1] Arnold's *English Works*, ii. 230.   [2] According to.

Christ that were suspended!"[1] Again, preaching
on "Two shall be in one bed; the one shall be
taken, and the other left," he says: "Some men live
contemplative lives, as these that rest in their bed,
and have oil of heavenly things; and all these shall
be saved. And some men live a thoughtful life,
and rest in their bed from works, but they think
not on heavenly things, or else they want devotion.
And such be many calculators, and astronomy
and other sciences. The first of these be taken to
Heaven, and the other be left to Hell."[2]

Our Reformer is certainly not here commending
an idle life, which he strongly censures in many
places, but is drawing a distinction between holy
meditations and vain thoughts. And whatever may
have moved him to speak thus hardly of scholarship,
it assuredly was not because he came short of it
himself. We must also remember what learned
folly much of the scholarship of his day was.

The Evangelical Doctor was quite conscious of
the progression and development of his views. "In
more than one place he makes the frankest ac-
knowledgment that on more than one metaphysical
question he had formerly defended with tenacity the
opposite of what he now maintained; that 'he was
sunk in the depths of the sea, and had stammered
out many things which he was unable clearly to
make good,' &c. But still more strongly does he
express himself in one of his unprinted writings,
where he makes the following free confession:—

---

[1] Arnold's *English Works*, i. 310.　　[2] *Ibid.*, ii. 408.

'Other statements which at one time appeared strange to me, now appear to me to be sound and true, and I defend them; for when I was a child in the knowledge of the faith I spake as a child, I understood as a child; but when in God's strength I became a man I put away by His grace childish thoughts.'"[1]

It is surprising to find on how many of the customs, the abuses, and the questions which interest men at this day, we are able to gather Wycliffe's thoughts. Do some of our modern clergy refuse to submit themselves to the judgment of the Civil Court? Our Reformer has some very trenchant words for them. "Our Saviour Jesus Christ suffered meekly painful death of Pilate, not excusing Him from his jurisdiction by His clergy"—*i.e.* "He did not claim benefit of clergy, the right to be tried by an ecclesiastical rather than a secular court."[2] The note is that of the Roman Catholic editor. "Who," exclaims Wycliffe a little further on, "hath made our worldly clerks exempt from kings' jurisdiction and chastising, since God giveth kings this office on all misdoers? Certainly no man but Antichrist, Christ's enemy; since clerks, and namely high priests, should be most meek and obedient to lords of this world, as were Christ and His apostles, and teach other men both in word and deed to be mirror of all men, to give this meekness and obedience to the King and his rightful laws. How strong

---

[1] Lechler's *Wiclif,* p. 253.
[2] Arnold's *English Works,* iii. 297.

thieves and traitors be they now to kings and lords in denying this obedience, and in giving example to all men in the land for to be rebels against the King and lords! For in this they teach unlearned men and commons of the land, both in words and laws and open deed, to be false and rebellious against the King and other lords."[1]

He has something to urge also against bishops "who swear to go and convert heathen men," and instead of fulfilling their vows, "dwell in England, and become rich bishops suffragans."[2]

For evolution, in the only form in which it was known to him,—namely, the idea that the soul of man first existed in the form of vegetable life, then in that of animal instinct, and lastly as an immortal spirit,— he has a word of contempt as he passes it by.[3]

Wycliffe distinctly contradicts the idea of conditional immortality, as becomes a man who takes his stand only on God's word. "All whole mankind, both saved men and damned, have being from Christ without end, but in two manners."[4] "Christ speaketh here thus to teach that punishment and sin must answer even, that the one be as long as the other; for this asketh God's righteousness."[5]

What has our Reformer to say on the latitudinarian notion that God might forgive sin without atonement? "It is a light word to say that God might of His power forgive this sin, without aseeth[6] that were

---

[1] Arnold's *English Works*, iii. 297, 298. [2] *Ibid.*, iii. 300.
[3] *Ibid.*, i. 369. [4] *Ibid.*, ii. 156. [5] *Ibid.*, ii. 175.
[6] Compensation, indemnity.

made for this trespass ; for God might do this if He
would, but His justice would not suffer that each
trespass be unpunished, either in earth or in Hell.
And God may [1] not accept persons, to forgive sin
without asceth, for else He must give free leave to
man and angel for to sin, and then sin were no sin,
and our God were no God." [2]

To us, accustomed to the historical and futurist
views of prophecy, it seems astonishing that Wycliffe
and other divines of his day should have calmly
assumed, as a matter of course, that the Millennium
was already over, and that they were living in the
after-period when Satan is to go forth to deceive the
nations. The Reformer frequently uses such terms
as " this came in when the fiend was loosed," or, " since
the loosing of the fiend such a thing has been done."
In his eyes the fiend was bound at the Advent, and
loosed in A.D. 1000. In the Reformation period this
was seen to be a mistake ; and the dates were moved
to the reign of Constantine and 1215. Wycliffe
regarded the thousand years not as a literal but a
mystical number.

Even trades unions and combinations to keep up
prices come under the lash of our Reformer's many-
thonged whip. " For they conspire together that no
man of their craft shall take less on a day that they
set, though he should by good conscience take much
less, and that none of them shall make sad [3] true work

---

[1] Wycliffe frequently uses *may* where a modern divine would
write *can.*

[2] Arnold's *English Works*, ii. 237.   [3] Serious, earnest.

to hinder other men's winning of the craft, and that none of them shall do aught but only hew stone, though he might profit his master twenty pound by laying[1] on a wall, without harm or paining himself. . . Also it seemeth that merchants, grocers, and victuallers run in the same curse fully. For they conspire wickedly together that none of them shall buy over a certain price, though the thing that they buy be much more worth, and they know well this ; and that none of them shall sell better cheap than another, though he may well afford it so, and it be not so much worth as another man's chaffer ; thus he shall be punished sore if he do true and good conscience."[2]

The scraps of scientific lore which Wycliffe scatters up and down his sermons are not without interest, as showing the state of general knowledge in his day, and in particular his own. He holds that earthquakes " come of winds closed within the earth," and pestilence " of distemper of elements, and of other mixed bodies that be unnaturally tempered ; for the fumes of these, blown with the winds, and drawn into man, distempereth his body, and maketh his humours and all his limbs to want their natural temper."[3] " Clerks say that salt is made of gravel and of water, with heat of the sun or of fire, and made hard with blast of the wind."[4] " The moon is mother of moist things."[5] " Waters that be above the moon be stable and clear

---

[1] Query whether the original word, "*leggyng*," ought to be rendered *laying*, i.e. mortaring, or whether it is satirical, and should be *lying ?*

[2] Arnold's *English Works*, iii. 333.   [3] *Ibid.*, i. 219.
[4] *Ibid.*, i. 267.   [5] *Ibid.*, ii. 177.

and everlasting; but waters that be beneath the moon, removing, frail, and partable. . . Under the moon is a sphere of subtle fire, and in that is a sphere of the air, and in either [*i. e.* both] sphere of the water, and in the middle of the world and lowest, sphere of the earth. . . . Clerks say that rain cometh thus: the planets, and especially the sun, draw up from the water and from other moist places a subtle body far into the air; and in the middle of the air is it naturally cooled by night, for this matter is by nature cold, and there wanteth heat of fire and light, and thus cold maketh this moist matter run together in small drops, and thus they get heaviness, and come down in form of rain. But sometimes these planets of heaven, against the time that the sun goeth down, lift up a subtle matter but a little space from the earth; and from the time the sun be hid, the cold of the night engrosseth this matter, and so it cometh down anon in more subtle form than rain. There lie many winds here; as some winds be in beasts, and some be closed within the earth, and some blown freely between the earth and stars of heaven. . . This wind is in his natural air mixed with water that cometh of the earth; and planets, with stars of heaven, and hurtling of clouds, move this wind now to one place, now to another, after the changing of the mover. . . . Snow . . holdeth heat within the earth, that it creep not out by small holes; and so it quickeneth the root of growing things within the earth. . . . Snow is gendered high in the air, when watery matter much in quantity to regard of the substance is frozen and

so falleth down, and hath whiteness for clear and
stable matter. . . . When clouds break by violence
that were fast together before, then they make a
great noise, which noise men call the thunder. . . .
In pores deep under the earth is waters gendered, . .
and water runneth in summer up cold earth, when
pores be open, therefore water commonly is more
cold in summer-time. In winter, when it is frost, the
pores of the earth are closed, . . therefore the water
that cometh by such pores hath heat in winter, and
smoke cometh out and welleth. . . When gravel is
hot with the sun, and soaked long with the water, it
taketh naturally a savour that men call saltness ; . .
the sea is commonly salt, for it taketh more the light
of heaven. . . . Beasts be subtler than be fishes in
their · shape, so they be more venomous, more an-
noyous unto man ; and thus fishes be near to [the]
elements, and more religious for to eat than be fowls
or beasts of earth, for they be near man's kind." [1]

With respect to passages of Scripture in the interpretation of which Christians differ, apart from any
questions of doctrine or discipline, we find that
Wycliffe's views were as follows. Doubtless in most
cases he followed the authorized interpretation of the
Church ; but not always, as we shall see.

The pearl of great price he explains to be Christ.[2]

He has no doubt of the identity of Mary of Bethany
with Mary Magdalene and the woman that was a
sinner.[3]

---

[1] Arnold's *English Works*, iii. 63—69.   [2] *Ibid.*, i. 286.
[3] *Ibid.*, ii. 114, 205.

Though he puts it as a supposition, yet he seems to think that John the Baptist sent his disciples to Christ for the confirmation of their faith, not of his own.[1]

On the difficult passage, " Thou art Peter, and on this rock will I build My Church," Wycliffe departs from the interpretation of the Roman See. " This corner-stone is Christ, of whom Peter hath his name ; and on this same stone is Holy Church grounded. And thus Peter and each man signifieth this stone."[2]

Of allegorizing interpretations, which he styled "mystical," he gives us many, doubtless taken in the main from the works of the Fathers. Wycliffe makes every parable "run on all fours" in a manner which would astonish some modern readers.

Let us take one entire parable — that of the labourers in the vineyard—and see what is made of it according to this remarkable process. It will help us to understand what were the best kind of sermons preached in Wycliffe's day.

The householder is God, and the vineyard is the Church. The penny a day is the Godhead and Manhood of Christ. (In the same manner he renders the two pence of the Good Samaritan.) The workmen are all the elect. The five hours that they stood idle (from the sixth to the eleventh ?) is the period from the creation to the birth of Christ. The vines are "true men "; the labour is preaching ; the steward is the manhood of Christ ; the evening is the judgment day. The grudging labourers are to be understood, with Pope Gregory, of the Old Testament saints, who

---

[1] Arnold's *English Works*, i. 71.   [2] *Ibid.*, i. 349.

"had merited Heaven by their good lives, yet obtained it not till the descent of Christ into hell had set them free, and opened to them the gates of Paradise." (This language is that of Gregory, not Wycliffe.) But Wycliffe strangely adds, " This deeming and grudging is wondering in soul, and *thanking* of God's grace, that He gave so much joy to men for so little travail !" [1]

Even a plain historical event, such as the marriage in Cana of Galilee, must have a " mystical" interpretation given to it. The wedding betokens the love of Christ to the Church ; the governor of the feast is the manhood of Christ ; the water-pots are Old Testament saints ; the water is the Law, the wine the Gospel.[2] So in Matt. xxiv., Judæa is confession ; the men who are in that province are priests ; those on the house-top are secular rulers, and they are not to come down, *i. e.* to fall from God's law ; men in the field are commoners, and they must not enter into the house, namely, turn from the truth for fear of worldly losses. Fleeing on the Sabbath day means overloading Sunday with ceremonies of man's invention.[3] Preaching on Mark vii. 31, about Christ going from the coasts of Tyre and Sidon through Decapolis to the Sea of Galilee, he stops to tell his hearers that Tyre signifies " making," and denotes Christ's going forth from the bosom of the Father ; that Sidon is " angelic," and intimates the service of angels to Christ ; that Galilee means " wheel," and prefigures

[1] Arnold's *English Works,* i. 98—101.   [2] *Ibid.,* i. 87.
[3] Ibid., ii. 398—400.

the incarnation, because man slid from innocence, and a wheel turns round! Men beguiled by Satan are the ten cities of Decapolis, by which Christ came on His journey, and so forth.[1]

Even the loaves and fishes must be allegorized. The loaves are the five books of Moses; the fishes "the books of Wisdom and the prophets, that be souel to these two loaves." The lad that had them in charge is Christ![2]

The net full of fishes that Peter drew to shore (John xxi.) has to be treated in like manner. The great number of fishes denotes the number of the saints resting (!) in the net, that is, Heaven; the three odd ones are the Holy Trinity! The hot coals on which the fishes were laid are the holy angels;—for what possible reason? Because they "burn in love of God, and feed others, and be fed"![3]

Surely such explanations as these must have come originally from men who had a vast quantity of time on their hands, and nothing good to do with it! That such a man as Wycliffe should calmly have accepted and repeated them is a psychological curiosity.

There was one groove of allegorical interpretation into which Wycliffe was sure to fall, for to avoid it he would have had to divest himself of all the ideas

---

[1] Arnold's *English Works*, i. 30.—Wycliffe draws his philology from Jerome, and it is often erroneous. Tyre really signifies *a rock*, and Sidon *fishing*.

[2] *Ibid.*, i. 63.—The old English word *souél* or *soül*, still extant in the north, will require explanation to some readers. It means anything savoury which forms a relish to bread. Its modern pronunciation in Lancashire is *saäl* or *sayal*. [3] *Ibid.*, ii. 138.

of his age. Such words as Zion, Jerusalem, Israel, &c., always to him mean the Church, without a shadow of supposition that there can be any primary and literal meaning at all. It was not until the Evangelical revival, born with the present century, that the possibility of a literal interpretation of such prophecies as Isaiah xlix. 22, or lx., dawned on the mind of universal Christendom.

Yet we find passages in Wycliffe's writings which show that he was not devoid of a preference for the plain literal meaning of Scripture rather than the allegorical,[1] and had he lived in a less mystical age he would probably have flung aside as useless trappings a great deal of this absurd system of interpretation.

Since Wycliffe and all his followers were accused of sedition, and charged by their enemies with preaching it, it is worth our while to see what political opinions they really held. The advanced Lollards of a somewhat later day were the Liberals, it may be said the Radicals, of their period. While they adhered fully to the monarchical principle, they wished to limit the power of the nobles, to destroy the hierarchy (by which is of course meant the office, not the men), and to disestablish and disendow the Church. They desired to see luxury decreased in all its forms, and their reverence for art was less than slight. They all wanted to do away with the religious Orders, with. the right of sanctuary, auricular confession, Latin services, superfluous ceremonies, images, indulgences, and clerical celibacy. On the questions of infant

[1] Lechler's *Wiclif*, pp. 274, 275.

baptism, forms of prayer, Church music, law, and war they differed ; some desiring to retain, and others to abolish them.

These were not altogether the political tenets of Wycliffe himself. He desired to see the Church disendowed, but not disestablished, and he would have been glad to get rid of the hierarchy. He had no reverence for art, for several times he reprobates all arts and luxuries which did not belong to the state of innocence. Infant baptism he would have retained, while Church music or much of it he would probably have done away with. Otherwise he sided mainly with his followers. His objection to endowments was entirely because he thought that they fostered a spirit of worldliness and pride in the clergy, which was eating out all spiritual energy among them. (Is this warning also not sorely needed now, when on all sides the clergy are yielding to the pressure of the richer and younger part of their flocks, in many cases against their own better judgment?) On two points, however, his opinions were certainly not those of the modern Radical. He was thoroughly loyal to his King,—the law of succession once constitutionally changed, he accepted the legal decision,—and he had no fancy whatever for mob law. The spirit of Thomas Carlyle might have rested for a moment in its flight downwards upon John Wycliffe, when we find him saying—

" Since there be few wise men, and fools be without number, assent of more part of men maketh evidence that it were folly. For as multitude of wise men is

[a] confirming of their deed, so more multitude of fools is evidence that they do evil."[1]

It does not sound like sedition to say, "Blessed be the Lord of Heaven, that keepeth much in [the] hands of secular lords!"[2] or, "Christ taught that God would that He obeyed thus to His king;"[3] or, "Since the King is God's vicar, dread ye God in His vicar."[4]

More strongly than this he writes in two of his most remarkable works, *The Seven Deadly Sins* and *The Great Sentence of Curse Expounded.*

"By the law of God they [the common people] should serve meekly to God and to their lords, and do true service to God and to their masters ; . . yea, by the law of Christ, if the lord be untrue man and tyrant to his subjects, yet should they serve him, for they should serve to God in meekness and charity. I have not read in God's law that subjects should fight with their worldly sovereigns, and so get them peace ; but Christ taught us by patience to vanquish our enemies and win the bliss of heaven, but not with other striving."[5]

"And when many lands should fall into the King's [hands], by escheat or other just means, these worldly clergy and vain religious [men] mede[6] greatly the King's officers and men of law, to forbear the King's right, and make themselves lords wrongfully. . . Also many worldly painted clerks get the King's

---

[1] Arnold's *English Works*, ii. 414.   [2] *Ibid.*, ii. 395.
[3] *Ibid.*, ii. 201.   [4] *Ibid.*, ii. 296.   [5] *Ibid.*, iii. 147.
[6] To reward, to pay fees, or give bribes.

P

seal, him outwitting, and send to Rome for benefices much gold; and when the King sendeth his privy seal for to advance good clerks, and able both of good life and great cunning [1] to rule, they bring forth hereby many worldly wretches, unable to rule one soul for default of cunning and good living, and thus use the King's seal against God's honour and the King's, and profit of Christian people, where [2] the King understandeth to do well by their suggestion. And therefore the King hath many cursed painted clerks about him, if he take heed to their life, cunning, and ruling of the Church." [3]   This was extremely true of two who were constantly about the King—Courtenay, Archbishop of Canterbury, and Bishop Arundel of Ely.

" Our King may lawfully take talliage [taxes] of the people, for needful help of the land." [4]

" Among all the men that ever were here in earth, none highed more than Christ secular lords; for He chose to be born when this lordship flourished most in the empire of Rome. Christ gave tribute to the Emperor; Christ would not so much lessen secular lordship that He would have a little house to hide His head in ; Christ commanded to give the Emperor that was his. . . And Christ nourished the tenants of secular lords ; He healed them and fed them, and robbed them not " [a side-hit at the friars]. [5]

---

[1] Knowledge, whether in the sense of wisdom or learning.
[2] In circumstances wherein.
[3] Arnold's *English Works*, iii. 307.
[4] *Ibid.*, iii. 320.   [5] *Ibid.*, iii. 435.

Whatever may be thought of the rather curious piece of argument in the last paragraph, we may surely acquit Wycliffe on the count of teaching sedition.

It must, however, be admitted that our Reformer held one very odd opinion, which his editor is pleased to term "ultra-Puritan." He may have come across Puritans who held it; I ask leave to say that I never did so. This was, that no person in authority, whether civil or ecclesiastical, held his power longer than during good behaviour. A king or a bishop who did not obey God's law had no right to the position he held! Nevertheless, as we have already seen, Wycliffe did not think that the subjects were to be the judges of this, far less the executioners.

On this point it is probable that Wycliffe has been much misunderstood—deliberately by his contemporaries and enemies, and accidentally by later commentators. Professor Burrows points out that the axiom of "dominion by grace" was simply one of those "paradoxical forms in which the schoolmen of the day were accustomed to present their conclusions",[1] and that it really meant no more than our familiar modern maxim that "Property has its duties as well as its rights."

A few words on the Reformer's style may be desirable. The English style is sufficiently shown by the extracts already given; but I must admit that I have chosen the plainest and most intelligible paragraphs, for in many places his wording, and still more his reasoning, is most difficult to follow. It

---

[1] *Wiclif's Place in History*, pp. 14, 16.

is hardly possible at times to see how he reaches his inference from his premises, and it is easier to agree with his conclusions than to understand how he came to them by the process of argument which he gives us. Much of this difficulty is no doubt due to our ignorance of the language and tone of thought of the period, rather than to any real obscurity on the part of the writer. He aimed at being understood by the common people, and we have abundant evidence that they did thoroughly understand him at the time.

The Latin writings of Wycliffe are at once barbarous and obscure. His German editors complain of his involved sentences and long paragraphs, and of the constant mixture of English idioms with the Latin ; while I have been told by a friend, that to any person accustomed to read elegant and classical Latin, that of Wycliffe "is simply blood-curdling"!

Of eloquent diction, in either language, there is very little to be found in the writings of the Reformer. In fact he deliberately avoided it—partly because he was too tremendously in earnest to save men to spend time in polishing up his sentences; and partly because he thought that such a study savoured of vain-glory,[1] and was not fit for Christian teachers. It is only when he is on fire with his subject, and his heart flows over into his tongue, that anything like beauty of language can be detected. Let us close the chapter with a specimen of these.

---

[1] Lechler's *Wiclif,* p. 207.

"Yea, the day of doom cometh full fast, since no time may come faster than this day cometh!"[1]

"'And they went forth, and kept with knights the sepulchre of Christ, marking the stone' that was put at the door in sight of the keeper, to mark their diligence. And thus do our high priests and our new religious [Orders]. They dread that God's law shall quicken after this, and therefore they make statutes, stable as a stone; and they get grants of knights to confirm them. And this they mark well, with witness of lords, lest that truth of God's law, hid in the sepulchre, burst out to knowledge of the common people. O Christ, Thy law is hid yet! when wilt Thou send Thine angel to remove the stone, and show Thy truth to Thy people? Well I know that knights took gold in this case, to help that Thy law be hid, and Thine ordinance cease, but well I know that it shall be known at the day of doom, or before, when Thou wilt, against all Thine enemies."[2]

[1] Arnold's *English Works*, i. 198.   [2] *Ibid.*, i. 129.

SUMMARY OF THE TENETS OF JOHN WYCLIFFE.

APPROVED.

Supreme authority of Holy Scripture.
Supreme headship of Christ over His Church.
Royal supremacy, civil and ecclesiastical.
Seven sacraments (but the two instituted by Christ pre-eminent).
Predestination, in the extremest sense.
Sabbath-keeping.
Infant baptism.
Use of sarcasm, in a good cause.

DISAPPROVED.

Doctrines.

Transubstantiation.
Power of the keys.
Exclusive priesthood of the clergy.
Mariolatry (late in life).
Image-worship (ditto).
Purgatory (ditto).
Apostolical succession.
Distinction between mortal and venial sins.
Baptismal regeneration.

Final perseverance.
Assurance.
Refusal of clergy to submit to civil courts.
Bishops appointed to heathen countries becoming suffragans in England.
Conditional immortality.
Socinian view of the Atonement.

Discipline.

Monasticism.
Endowments.
Papal Bulls and Decretals.

Tradition.
Auricular confession.
Clerical celibacy.

Religious Practices.

Indulgences.
Begging by friars.
Simony (in which he included selling of advowsons, bribes for promotions, consecration and marriage fees, &c.).
Fasting communion.
Letters of fraternity ("selling prayers").
Dying in monk's habit.
Canonization.

Intoning, and *much* music of any kind.
Incense.
Latin services.
Family chaplains.
Costly churches and abbeys.
Consecration of places.
Washing feet of poor on Maundy Thursday.
Holy water.
Pilgrimages.

Secular Practices.

Drunkenness and greediness.
Dress and luxury.
Amusements (tournaments, archery, wrestling, plays, chess, and backgammon are named).
Dinner-parties.
Guilds and societies.

Freemasons.
War.
Law-suits.
Secular learning.
Trades unions.
Government by majorities.
Combinations to keep up prices.

INDEX.

Tales of English Life in the Olden Time.

By EMILY S. HOLT.

WEARYHOLME; Or, SEEDTIME AND HARVEST.

Crown 8vo, 5/-.

" The characters are ably drawn, and a most interesting as well as instructive work is thus provided."—*Rock.*

Lady Sibyl's Choice.

A Tale of the Crusades. Crown 8vo, 5/-.

"The book charms from the naïve simplicity of the heroine and from the skill with which the authoress has preserved the spirit of the age."
The Graphic.

Red and White.

A Tale of the Wars of the Roses. Crown 8vo, 5/-.

" A charming historical Tale, full of clever portraiture and antique colouring."—*Publishers' Circular.*
" The whole story is well conceived and spiritedly told."—*Guardian.*

Margery's Son;

Or, Until He Find It. A Story of the Court of Scotland. 5/-.

" Carefully studied and well written. The story is admirably told."
British Quarterly Review.

Robin Tremayne.

A Tale of the Marian Persecution. Crown 8vo, 5/-.

" The book is extremely well written."
Athenæum.

Lettice Eden;

Or, The Lamps of Earth and the Light of Heaven. Cr. 8vo, 5/-.

" We promise its readers a rare literary feast."—*The Christian.*

Isoult Barry of Wynscote.

A Tale of Tudor Times. 5/-.

" The book is as charming as it is profitable."—*The Christian.*

The White Rose of Langley.

A Story of the Court of England in the Olden Time. Crown 8vo, 5/-.

" An admirable, instructive, and very interesting volume."
English Independent.

Verena;

Or, Safe Paths and Slippery Byeways. A Story of To-day. 5/-.

" The naturalness and brightness of the dialogue forms the charm of the story."—*City Press.*

Ashcliffe Hall.

A Tale of the Last Century. 5/-.

" It is able and natural, well written and thoroughly entertaining from beginning to end."—*Record.*

Clare Avery.

A Story of the Spanish Armada. Crown 8vo, 5/-.

" An admirable story, full of life and vigour."—*Rock.*

Imogen.

A Story of the Mission of St. Augustine. Crown 8vo, 5/-.

" Illustrates with equal beauty and fidelity the characteristics of an eventful period of our history."—*Record.*

Joyce Morrell's Harvest;

Or, THE ANNALS OF SELWICK HALL. Crown 8vo, 5/-.

" These chronicles are full of good things, which are sure to be as precious seed in the heart of any young person into whose hands they may come."
The Congregationalist.

LONDON : JOHN F. SHAW & CO., 48, PATERNOSTER ROW, E.C.

𝔖torics for all 𝔄ges

JOHN ∴ F.∴ SHAW ∴ AND ∴ CO.

48, PATERNOSTER ROW, LONDON, E.C.,

AND SOLD BY ALL BOOKSELLERS.

*** COMPLETE CATALOGUES SENT POST-FREE ON APPLICATION.

"Messrs. J. F. SHAW & Co. *having established a specialité in their books of fiction drawn from the facts of history in the past, and the facts of Christian life and work in the present, can always reckon upon a public for their Gift Books, and their recent issues will more than sustain their reputation."*—PUBLISHERS' CIRCULAR.

SHAW'S HOME SERIES.

Price SIXPENCE each, with Coloured Illustrated Wrapper.

THE need of providing cheap but good reading for the many who are yearly passing out of our Sunday and Day Schools is increasingly felt; and it is hoped this Series will do something to meet it.

For convenience of size, legibility, and attractiveness it is superior to any of the recent cheap issues, while the popularity of the three first is too well assured to need more than the mention of their Titles and Authors.

No. 1.—FROGGY'S LITTLE BROTHER. By BRENDA.

No. 2.—SCAMP AND I. By L. T. MEADE.

No. 3.—MISTRESS MARGERY. By EMILY S. HOLT.

To be followed by others.

NEW ILLUSTRATED STORIES.

ALL PLAY. By ISMAY THORN.

With Title, Initial Letters, and numerous Illustrations by T. PYM. Cloth extra, 3/6.

A book that will delight the little ones. The story is bright and childlike in its naturalness, and rendered most attractive by the charming and numerous illustrations with which it is adorned.

INGLE-NOOK STORIES. By Mrs. STANLEY LEATHES.

With numerous Ilustrations by M. IRVINE. Square, cloth extra, 2/6.

Full of pleasant things for the little ones, these stories will afford many a happy half-hour as they are read and talked about by the critical and interested juveniles.

OUR DARLINGS.

Containing splendid Coloured Illustrations, Pictures on every page, and Attractive Stories, in brilliantly-executed Coloured Boards, price 3/-; cloth extra gilt, gilt edges, price 5/-

Edited by Dr. BARNARDO.

The most attractive children's volume of the season.

Catalogue B.   (1)

(3)

BRENDA'S STORIES.

Little Cousins;
Or, Georgie's Visit to Lotty.
With Illustrations by T. PYM.
Square, cloth, 3/6.

"The illustrations are pretty, and add much to the attractiveness of the book, which is one sure to satisfy any little girl to whom it may be given."
Athenæum.

Victoria Bess;
Or, The Ups and Downs of a Doll's Life. With Illustrations by T. PYM. Square, cloth, 3/6.

"A charming little book for little girls, told with just a touch of humour and abundance of gentle pathos."
Literary World.

A Saturday's Bairn.
With Illustrations. New Edition.
Crown 8vo, cloth, 5/-.

"A charming tale, over which smiles and tears contend."—*Christian World.*
"An admirable story."—*Court Journal.*

Lotty's Visit to Grandmama.
A Story for the Little Ones.
With Fifty Illustrations by W. J. PETHERICK. Small 8vo, cloth, 3/6.

"An admirable book for little people. We most cordially recommend parents and others on the look out for the replenishment of the children's book-shelf to get this."—*Literary World.*

Nothing to Nobody.
With Illustrations. New Edition.
Small 8vo, cloth, 2/6.

"A very pretty story, and will serve as a gift-book, either for rich children or poor ; both will find something to interest them."—*Athenæum.*

Froggy's Little Brother.
A Story of the East End. With Eight Illustrations by "CAs." New Edition. Small 8vo, cloth, 3/6.

"Has an individuality and beauty of its own which makes it very pathetic and yet comical reading."—*Guardian.*

STORIES OF OUR CITY WAIFS.

"Ragamuffins;"
Or, The Arabs of Love Lane.
By JESSIE SALE LLOYD. 2/6.

"A cleverly written lively tale full of incident and interest."—*Record.*

Wilfred.
A Story with a Happy Ending.
By A. T. WINTHROP. 3/6.

"This charming and touching story will fascinate all who come under its influence."—*Freeman.*

All Among the Daisies.
By Mrs. STANLEY LEATHES.
Small 8vo, 2/6.

"Young readers, and many readers who can scarcely call themselves young, will be delighted with the work. It deserves high praise."—*The Scotsman.*

Gipsy Mike; Or, FIRM AS A ROCK.
With Illustrations. Crown 8vo, 3/6.
"This very touching and well-written book."—*Standard.*
"A touching story of self-sacrifice."
Record.

JACK AND JILL.
A Story of To-day. By Mrs. STANLEY LEATHES, Author of "All Among the Daisies," &c. With Illustrations. Small 8vo, 2/6.

"A charming little story."—*Record.*
"Some of the incidents are extremely moving."—*Times.*
"Charmingly written and illustrated."—*Watchman.*

LITTLE FREDDIE; Or, FRIENDS IN NEED.
By E. E. G. With Illustrations. Small 8vo, cloth extra, 2/6.

"This very touching story, well worked out."—*Guardian.*
"There is real pathos in this story, telling how a poor little waif is protected from evil by the recollection of a lost mother's teaching."—*Liverpool Courier.*

LONDON: JOHN F. SHAW & CO., 48, PATERNOSTER ROW, E.O.

CHAPTERS IN OUR "ISLAND STORY."

By L. E. GUERNSEY.

THE FOSTER SISTERS.

A Story of the Great Revival. Crown 8vo, cloth extra, 5/-

"A pretty story of the last century; the style is bright and sparkling."—*Athenæum.*
"Can be highly recommended as a present to girls."—*Standard.*
"The story is charmingly told."—*Guardian.*

The Chevalier's Daughter.

Or, An Exile for the Truth. 5/-
"One of those quaint old-world stories which the author knows so well how to write."—*Leeds Mercury.*

Lady Betty's Governess;

Or, THE CORBET CHRONICLES. 5/-
"An unusually successful attempt to reproduce the manners of the 17th century. The book, which is well and simply written, will give pleasure to its readers."
Saturday Review.

Lady Rosamond's Book;

Or, Dawnings of Light. Crown 8vo, cloth, 5/-.
"A well-told story, written in quaint old-time style, the plot interesting and well sustained, and the tone good."
Leeds Mercury.

Winifred.

An English Maiden of the Seventeenth Century. Crown 8vo, 3/6.
"A truly delightful story, drawn the life.'—*Leeds Mercury.*

The Earl Printer.

A Tale of the Time of Caxton. Illustrated. Cloth, 2/6.
A welcome picture of the times of the great master printer."
Daily Review.

The Sword of De Bardwell.

A Tale of Agincourt. By C. M. K. PHIPPS. Small 8vo, 2/6.
From an old inscription, the author has written an interesting narrative of this part of our "rough island story."

GEOFFREY THE LOLLARD.

By F. EASTWOOD. New Edition, with illustrations, cloth, 3/6.
"Will fascinate any into whose hands the tale is placed."—*Christian World.*

By Rev. ANDREW REED.

EDGAR NELTHORPE;

Or, THE FAIR MAIDS OF TAUNTON. Crown 8vo, cloth extra, 6/-.
"It is very well done, with an earnest, moral purpose."—*The Scotsman.*

Alice Bridge, of Norwich.

A Tale of the Time of Charles I. Crown 8vo, cloth, 6/-.
"Well adapted to give a clearer perception of a period that has passed away."—*English Independent.*

Ida Vane.

A Tale of the Restoration. Crown 8vo, 6/-.
"A delightfully written book; there is scarcely a dull page in it."
Scotsman.

"**These volumes give a wonderfully clear and graphic picture of social and religious life in the troublous times immediately before and after the Restoration.**"—*Watchman.*

LONDON: JOHN F. SHAW & CO., 48, PATERNOSTER ROW, E.C.

POPULAR HOME STORIES.

By EMILY BRODIE.

NORA CLINTON;

Or, DID I DO RIGHT? Crown 8vo, cloth extra, 3/6.

The pleasant pen of Miss Brodie has been well employed in this earnest story. Young hearts will be steadied and strengthened by the lessons so lovingly enforced.

Lonely Jack and his Friends at Sunnyside. Crown 8vo, 3/6.
" Its chapters will be eagerly devoured by the reader."—*Christian World.*

The Hamiltons; or, Dora's Choice. Crown 8vo, 3/6.
"Miss Brodie's stories have that savour of religious influence and teaching which makes them valuable as companions of the home."—*Congregationalist.*

Uncle Fred's Shilling: Its Travels and Adventures. Crown 8vo, 3/6.
"Children will follow it with as eager interest as the little people who listened to it in the book itself, and learn all unconsciously many valuable lessons."
Christian World.

Jean Lindsay, the Vicar's Daughter. Crown 8vo, 3/6.
"The tale is admirably told, and some capital engravings interpret its principal incidents."—*Bookseller.*

Elsie Gordon; Or, Through Thorny Paths. Crown 8vo, 3/6.
"The characters have been well thought out. We are sure the volume will be welcome at many a fireside."—*Daily Express*

Ruth's Rescue; or, The Light of Ned's Home. Small 8vo, cloth, 1/-

Rough the Terrier. His Life and Adventures. Illustrated. Sq. 2/6.
"A clever autobiography, cleverly illustrated."—*The Christian.*

Aunt Hester, & Why we Loved her. A Story of Rosebrook. Crown 8vo, cloth, 3/6.
"This charmingly fresh and original story."—*Literary World.*
"A good book for boys charmingly written."—*Church of England Sunday School Magazine.*

Elsie's Santa Claus. With Illustrations. Cloth, 3/6.
"A charming Christmas story."
English Independent.

Prairie Days; Or, Our Home in the Far West. By M. B. SLEIGHT. With Illustrations. Crown 8vo, cloth, 5/-.
"Parents will find this a capital book to read to the children when assembled round during the long winter evenings."
Literary World.

Minnie Grey; Or, For Conscience' Sake. New Edition. Cloth, 2/6.
"A pleasing, well-written tale. Deserves hearty commendation."—*Record.*

RIDLEY'S BOOKS FOR BOYS.

WALTER ALISON: His Friends and Foes. By M. L. RIDLEY, Author of "Our Captain," "The Three Chums." With Illustrations. Crown 8vo, cloth extra, 3/6.

OUR CAPTAIN. The Heroes of Barton School. With Illustrations. New Edition. Crown 8vo, cloth extra, 3/6.
"A first-class book for boys."—*Daily Review.* | "A regular boy's book."—*Christian World.*

THE THREE CHUMS. A Story of School Life. Crown 8vo, 3/6.
"The story is well told, and the incidents are full of school-life: it is a book after a boy's heart. How can we better commend it than by saying it is both manly and godly?"—Rev. C. H. SPURGEON in *Sword and Trowel.*

LONDON: JOHN F. SHAW & CO., 48, PATERNOSTER ROW, E.O.

STORIES BY L. T. MEADE,

Author of " Scamp and I," &c.

GREAT ST. BENEDICT'S.

A TALE.

New Edition. Crown 8vo, cloth, with Illustrations, 6/-.

"The description of Dorothy's life is excellent."—*Spectator.*

" At once a noble book, and a most interesting story."—*Court Circular.*

"We have read this admirably-conceived and powerfully-written tale with extreme interest. It is so much above its class, that we cannot speak too highly of it for family reading."—*The Christian.*

Water Gipsies. A Tale.

Crown 8vo, cloth, 3/6.

" It is full of incident from beginning to end, and we do not know the person who will not be interested in it."
Christian World.

David's Little Lad.

Crown 8vo, cloth, 3/6.

"A finely-imagined story, bringing out in grand relief the contrast between quiet, steady self-sacrifice and brilliant, flashy qualities."—*Guardian.*

Your Brother and Mine.

A Cry from the Great City. Illustrated. Cloth, 2/6.

" A story of intense power and pathos, sketching the career of one of the little waifs and strays of our great cities, and his rescue, by the loving effort of a child."

Dot and Her Treasures. A Tale.

With Illustrations. Small 8vo, 2/6.

"One of the tales of poor children in London, of which we have had many examples; but none finer, more pathetic, or more original than this."
Nonconformist.

Lettie's Last Home. Cloth, 1/6.

" Very touchingly told."
Aunt Judy's Magazine.

White Lilies, and other Tales.

With Illustrations. Cloth, 1/6.

" Stories of a singularly touching and beautiful character."—*Rock.*

A Knight of To-day. A Tale.

New Edition. With Illustrations. Crown 8vo, cloth, 6/-

"A finely-imagined story of a good man. It is a book well worth reading.'
The Guardian.

"The author has appropriately dedicated the volume to Charles Kingsley. It is praise to say the book is not unworthy of the dedication."—*Athenæum.*

The Children's Kingdom ;

Or, The Story of a Great Endeavour. Crown 8vo, cloth, 5/-

"A really well-written story, with many touching passages. Boys and girls will read it with eagerness and profit."
The Churchman.

Bel-Marjory. A Tale.

New Edition. Cr. 8vo, cloth, 6/-

" Most interesting ; we give it our hearty commendation."—*English Independent.*

"Full of pathos, sh wing a thorough insight into the intricacies of human character. Miss Meade tells a well-conceived tale in a most able and effective manner."—*Leeds Mercury*

SCAMP AND I.

A Story of City Byeways. New Edition. With Illustrations.
Crown 8vo, cloth, 3/6.

" Little Flo', with her industry and skill, her motherly instincts and efforts to keep her young brother Dick, the crossing-sweeper, honest ; the good-natured, agreeable, clever young thief Jenks ; and, above all, the dear dog Scamp, with his knowing ways and soft brown eyes, are all as true to life and as touchingly set forth as any heart could desire."—*Athenæum.*

LONDON: JOHN F. SHAW & CO., 48, PATERNOSTER ROW, E.C.

HELPFUL STORIES FOR ELDER GIRLS.

BEK'S FIRST CORNER, AND HOW SHE TURNED IT.
By J. M. CONKLIN, Author of "Out in God's World."
Crown 8vo, 5/-
A charming story for elder girls.

OUT IN GOD'S WORLD;
Or, ELECTA'S STORY. By J. M. CONKLIN. Crown 8vo, cloth extra, 5/-.

"One of the most touching and elevating stories we have read. From beginning to end the tale is enchanting."—*Daily Review.*

THE LIGHT OF THE HOME;
Or, MABEL'S STORY. By Author of "Aunt Hester, & Why we loved her."
Crown 8vo, cloth extra, 5/-.

"It is a delightfully-told story, and will be one of the most popular girls' books of the season."—*The Standard.*

True to the End.
The Story of a Sister's Love. By Rev. Dr. EDERSHEIM. 3/6.
"An interesting story."—*Rock.*

Moore's Forge.
A Tale of Work for the Master. Small 8vo, Illustrated, cloth, 3/6.
"Just the kind of story to be read, enjoyed, and thought about."—*Rock.*

The Lost Jewel. A Tale.
By A. L. O. E. New Edition, with Illustrations, cloth, 3/6.
"Most heartily do we recommend our readers to place it in their libraries."
British Mothers' Journal.

Ella's Half-Sovereign;
Or, Pains and Gains. Crown 8vo, 3/6.
"We have really enjoyed this wise, bright story."—*Christian World.*

The Odd One;
Or, The Niche for Me to Fill. Cloth, 3/6.
"Will certainly be read with pleasure."—*English Independent.*

The Old House on Briar Hill.
By I. G MEREDITH. A Real Girl's Book. 3/6.
"Full of bright, wise precepts. A charming work."—*Christian World.*

MARION SCATTERTHWAITE.
A Story of Work. By MAGGIE SYMINGTON.
Crown 8vo, cloth extra, 6/-

"Contains a good deal of good writing and of sound teaching. No young reader will read it without being interested in it."—*The Scotsman.*

"SEEKETH NOT HER OWN;"
Or, THE WORKERS OF LA GARAYE. By M. SITWELL. Crown 8vo, cloth extra, 3/6.

"A strikingly effective narrative of a life of self sacrifice."—*Liverpool Courier.*

LONDON: JOHN F. SHAW & CO., 48, PATERNOSTER ROW, E.C.

(10)

Books Suitable for Sunday School Rewards.

CRIPPLE JESS, THE HOP PICKER'S DAUGHTER.

By L. Marston, Author of "Rob and Mag." Small 8vo, cloth extra, 2/6.

"A charming story."—*Record.*
"Fully as engrossing as anything from the pen of Hesba Stretton."—*The Christian.*
"A sketch well drawn of a sweet flower blooming in a very humble place."
Woman's Work.

Frank Usher;
Or, Soldiers of the Cross. Small 8vo. 2/6.
"Readable and instructive."
Aunt Judy's Magazine.

Christine; or, The Bible Girl. By S. Punot. Cloth. 2/6.
"Its exceeding naturalness and pathos."
Christian World.

Nellie's Secret;
Or, Brown's Alley and Sunny-side. By M. M. Pollard. 2/6.
"An excellent Sunday-school prize."
Record.

Flower Stories for Little Gatherers. Small 8vo. Cloth, 2/6.
"Peculiarly pleasing and profitable."
Christian Age.

His Grandchild.
A Tale of North Harbour. By M. M. Pollard. Cloth, 2/6.
"A wholesome and interesting story."
Rock.

Little Freddie; or, Friends in Need.
By E. G. Small 8vo, 2/6.
"A very touching little story well worked out."—*Guardian.*

HIS MOTHER'S BOOK;

By the Author of "Little Freddie." Small 8vo, cloth extra, 2/6.

Not a few stories have sketched the blessed influences of the Parent's Bible on the child, but seldom has it been portrayed more touchingly than in the story of "Bill and His Master." The volume will form a most suitable Sunday School reward.

John F. Shaw & Co.'s New Shilling Series,

IN VERY ATTRACTIVE BINDINGS, WITH ILLUSTRATIONS.

Chick; or, Yet there is Room. By M. S. MacRitchie.
Out in the Storm; or, Little Messengers. By Catharine Shaw.
Ruth's Rescue; or, The Light of Ned's Home. By Emily Brodie.
Rob and Ralph; or, A Trust Fulfilled.
Lonely Lily; or, The Shepherd's Call.
The New School; or, We Got Agate of Singing.
Lucy's Life Story; or, Sunshine Without and Within.
Twice Found; or, The Heavenly and the Earthly Father.
Terry; or, Trying to Follow. By L. E. D.
Thady March; or, The Story of My Boyhood.
Little Oranges; or, A Friend for the Friendless. By J. Harrison.

By L. Marston, Author of "Cripple Jess," &c.

Blind Nettie; or, Seeking her Fortune.
Benny, the King's Little Servant.

LONDON: JOHN F. SHAW & CO., 48, PATERNOSTER ROW, E.C

Eighteenpenny Present Books

FOR BOYS AND GIRLS.
IN ATTRACTIVE BINDINGS, WITH ILLUSTRATIONS.

By EMILY S. HOLT, Author of "Mistress Margery," &c.

The Way of the Cross. A Tale of the Early Church.

Hettie; or, Not Forsaken. By F. M. SAVILL.

Lost Her Shoe and other Threads. By GRACE STEBBING.
The "threads" alluded to in the title are threads of unselfishness, on which noble quality all the tales in this little volume are more or less distinctly founded.

A Little Wild Flower;
Or, Rosy's Story. By L. J. TOMLINSON.

Peggy's Charge. By the Author of "Polly and Winnie."

Sam. The Story of a Little While. By ISMAY THORN.

Rob and Mag.
A Little Light in a Dark Corner. By L. MARSTON.

On the Doorsteps;
Or, Crispin's Story. By Mrs. STANLEY LEATHES.

"Those Boys."
A Story for all Little Fellows. By AUNT PENN.

Jamie's Trust;
Or, The Motherless Bairn. Edited by H. K. F. GATTY.

"Keeping Open House."
By MARY W. McLAIN.

The Young Armour Bearer;
Or, Chosen to be a Soldier.

Little Trouble the House.
By AUNT PENN.

Harold;
Or, Following the Footprints.

Tom Knight;
Or, Who Gives True Honour.

Pop and Peggy;
or, How Tom was Rescued.

By M. L. C., Author of "Lonely Lily."

Left at Home;
The Heart's True Resting Place.

The Happy Land;
Or, Willie the Orphan.

Wandering May;
Or, Come Unto Me.

Clarie's Little Charge.
New Edition.

Charlie and Lucy;
Or, The Lonely Heart made Glad.

Tom Carter;
Or, Ups and Downs in Life.

Astray and at Home;
Or, Little Mollie and her Brother.

Polly and Winnie;
The Story of the Good Samaritan.

Old David's Lassie;
Or, Lost and Found.

Willow Bank; or, Only a Week.

May Lane; or, Love and Duty.

Little Nan;
Or, A Living Remembrance.

These volumes will be found most suitable for Sunday-school Rewards and Libraries. The Stories are full of interest, and their tone and tendency unexceptionable.

LONDON: JOHN F. SHAW & CO., 48, PATERNOSTER ROW, E.C.

(13)

Books for Sunday Reading.

MARJORIE'S PROBATION.

Chapters from a Life Story. By J. S. Ranking. Cr. 8vo, cloth extra, 3 6.

Earnest, loving, and tender, these chapters will bless many more than the heroine to whom they were originally told. Elder girls will both enjoy it and profit by it.

LIVING WATER FOR LITTLE PITCHERS.

By Rev. James Stephens. Crown 8vo, cloth extra, 3/-

"Admirably suited to the purpose for which they are intended, short, and animated, full of anecdote, and certain not only to retain the attention but to appeal to the affections of young readers."—*Guardian.*

Only a Tramp.

By Grace Stebbing, Author of "Silverdale Rectory," &c. With Illustrations. Crown 8vo, cloth extra, 3/6.

"Miss Stebbing holds the attention and extorts the admiration of the reader from first to last. Her able delineations of character, and breezy descriptions of country ways and scenes, help to brighten her pages, from which may be learnt many a weighty lesson."—*The Christian.*

Little Boots, And the Steps they Trod In.

By J. Harrison, Author of "The Boy's Watchword." Cloth, 2/6.

"A beautiful story of a mother's training of her boy."—*Watchman.*

Little Boots Grown Older;

Or, The Soldier of the Cross. Cloth, 2/6.

"Teachers and elder scholars may read the book with profit."
Wesleyan Sunday School Magazine.

Marcella of Rome.

A Tale of the Early Church. By F. Eastwood. Small 8vo. Illustrated. Cloth, 3/6.

"Will be an acceptable present, and form a useful addition to the books suitable for Sunday."—*Athenæum.*

Every Day Battles.

Or, Fighting the Foe. New Edition. Crown 8vo, 5/-. Illustrated.

"Pleasant reading for families. Some young people will be charmed with this book."—*Sword and Trowel.*

Tim's Little Mother.

By S. Punot. With Illustrations. New Edition. Cloth, 3/6.

"An affecting, unaffected story of London life."—*The Christian.*

Leoline; or, Captured & Rescued.

A Story for the Young. By Emily Grace Harding. With Illustrations. Cloth, 2/6.

"A very simply-written and interesting story."—*Yorkshire Post.*

Silverdale Rectory;

Or, The Golden Links. By Grace Stebbing. With Illustrations. Crown 8vo, 3/6.

"We can heartily recommend this story. It shows how the beautiful words in our morning and evening service may help us if we only realize them and make them our own."—*Church of England Sunday School Magazine.*

The Story of Martin Luther

Edited by Miss Whately. Seventh Edition. Cloth extra, 5/-.

"Should find a place in every school or parochial library."—*The Bookseller.*

Marty and the Mite Boxes;

Or, Boy Life and Boy Work. By J. Harrison. Illustrated. Cloth, 3/6.

"A capital book for boys—the style taking, and the whole teaching thoroughly wholesome."—*Watchman.*

Silent Highways.

A Story of Barge Life. By C. Palmer, Author of "Dogged Jack," &c. Small 8vo, cloth extra, 2/6.

"An affecting story, splendidly told."
Daily Review.

"It is extremely interesting."

Nobody's Lad.

The Scotsman.

By Leslie Keith. With Illustrations by Petherick. Crown 8vo, 3/6.

"We have seldom read anything to equal this story in deep pathos and earnestness of purpose."—*The Christian.*

LONDON: JOHN F. SHAW & CO., 48, PATERNOSTER ROW, E.C.

CAPITAL BOOKS FOR BOYS.

QUEER PETS AND THEIR DOINGS.

By OLIVE THORNE MILLER. Fully Illustrated.

4to, cloth extra, gilt edges, 7/6.

"Those who delight to hear of the ways and doings, the manners and customs, of birds and beasts, will spend some happy hours in company with 'Queer Pets.'"

Dublin Daily Express.

LITTLE FOLKS IN FEATHERS AND FUR,
AND OTHERS IN NEITHER.

By OLIVE THORNE MILLER. With nearly 200 Illustrations.

Cloth extra, gilt edges, 7/6.

"A delightful volume for young people."—*Court Journal.*
"A charming book, which in attractiveness for little folks will vie successfully with many a collection of fairy tales."—*English Independent.*

GOLD AND GLORY;

Or, Wild Ways of Other Days. By GRACE STEBBING, Author of "Brave Geordie," &c. With Illustrations. Cr. 8vo, cloth extra, 5/-

"We can cordially recommend this to all youthful lovers of adventure and enterprise."—*Academy.*
"A hero that boys will delight in."—*St. James' Gazette.*

GARRICK; OR, HIS OWN FAULT.

By YOTTY OSBORN. With Illustrations. Crown 8vo, cloth extra.

"Will be a favourite, and deservedly so."—*Guardian.*
"Such a book is invaluable, teaching as fine a lesson as any sermon."

Literary World.

HUBERT D'ARCY, THE YOUNG CRUSADER.

With Illustrations. Crown 8vo, cloth extra, 5/-

"This capital story."—*Standard.*
"Full of stirring adventure and desperate perils."—*Guardian.*

THE LYONS' DEN & ITS EIGHT YOUNG LYONS.

By YOTTY OSBORN, Author of "Jack," "Pickles,"&c. With Illustrations.

Crown 8vo, cloth extra, 5/-.

"An exceptionally good children's story; it brims over with fun, but has notwithstanding a substratum of sound good sense."—*Glasgow Herald.*
"Into the 'Den' we peep, and would gladly linger with its inmates."—*Athenæum.*

Brave Geordie.

The Story of an English Boy. By GRACE STEBBING. With Illustrations. Crown 8vo, cloth, 3/6.

"It is refreshing to meet with such a spirited and thoroughly good story."

The Christian.

The House in the Glen,

And the Boys who built it. Crown 8vo. Illustrated. Cloth, 3/6.

"Exactly what boys like. It looks at the world from their level, and is at the same time full of the spirit that is best for them."—*Guardian.*

Jack. A Chapter in a Boy's Life.

By Y.OSBORN,Author of 'Pickles,' &c. With Illustrations by PETHERICK, 5/-.

"We have seldom met with a more life-like portrait of an honest manly school-boy than that of Jack."

Christian World.

Basil Grey; or, Tried and True.

By Rev. W. J. BETTISON. Illustrated. Cloth, 2/6.

"A thoroughly good and hearty story for boys, we heartily recommend it."

Freeman.

LONDON: JOHN F. SHAW & CO., 48, PATERNOSTER ROW, E.O.

NEW & ATTRACTIVE STORIES.

Wearyholme; or, Seedtime and Harvest. By EMILY S. HOLT. Crown 8vo, 5/-

This favourite writer here depicts the eventful period of the Restoration, and shows most vividly the true principle which inspired many earnest spirits among both parties during that changeful time.

Bek's First Corner, and How She Turned It.

By J. M. CONKLIN, Author of "Out in God's World." Crown 8vo, 5/-
A charming story for elder girls, sketching most helpfully and naturally the first years of home life, when the hopes and expectations of the school time are exchanged for the experience and discipline of actual life.

Winning an Empire. By GRACE STEBBING, Author of "Gold and Glory." Crown 8vo, 5/-

The life of CLIVE gives a wonderful instance of the victory to be won over circumstances by force of character. In "Winning an Empire" the founder of our dominion in India presents himself in all the brilliancy of his own great doings to the reader.

The Robber Chief; or, Too Good for his Trade. By EDWARD BURTON. Crown 8vo, 3/6.

Another of those tales of wild deeds and magnanimity that never fail to please boys, and girls too, whether the scene be laid in the Deserts of Africa, the Prairies of America, or, as in the present instance, in the Scottish Highlands.

The Caged Linnet; or, Love's Labour not Lost. By Mrs. STANLEY LEATHES, Author of "Jack and Gill." Crown 8vo, 3/6.

The genial influence of a loving child on the soured and crabbed spirit of an older relative is beautifully depicted in this touching story.

Walter Alison: His Friends and Foes. By M. L. RIDLEY, Author of "The Three Chums." Crown 8vo, 3/6.

Another capital boy's story from the author of "The Three Chums," of which Mr. Spurgeon wrote, in "Sword and Trowel," "It is a book after a boy's heart. How can we better commend it than by saying that it is both manly and godly?"

The Emperor's Boys. By ISMAY THORN. Crown 8vo, 3/6.

A boy's story of no common merit, in which the elements of a true and noble manhood are strikingly brought out in contrast with their opposites. Boys will like it, and it will do them good.

Alick's Hero. By CATHARINE SHAW, Author of "Only a Cousin," &c. Crown 8vo, 3/6.

We are sure many a mother who has rejoiced to see her daughters influenced and helped by this author's tales will thank her for remembering the eager lads, and seeking to win them to all that is noble and good by this story of a true hero.

Nora Clinton; or, Did I Do Right? By EMILY BRODIE, Author of "Uncle Fred's Shilling," &c. Cr. 8vo, 3/6.

The pleasant pen of Miss Brodie has been well employed in this earnest story. Young hearts will be steadied and strengthened by the lessons so lovingly enforced.

"Messrs. JOHN F. SHAW & Co. have produced an admirable Series of Gift Books suited to all ages, and possessing in common the characteristics of attractiveness of binding, clearness of type, liberality of illustration, and excellence of matter."—*The Guardian.*

LONDON: JOHN F. SHAW & CO., 48, PATERNOSTER ROW, E.C.

www.ingramcontent.com/pod-product-compliance
Lightning Source LLC
Chambersburg PA
CBHW020108030726
47498CB00006B/2005